TYLER

BROTHERHOOD PROTECTORS WORLD

GUARDIAN AGENCY
BOOK SEVEN

REGAN BLACK

BROTHERHOOD PROTECTORS
ORIGINAL SERIES BY ELLE JAMES

Brotherhood Protectors Series

Montana SEAL (#1)

Bride Protector SEAL (#2)

Montana D-Force (#3)

Cowboy D-Force (#4)

Montana Ranger (#5)

Montana Dog Soldier (#6)

Montana SEAL Daddy (#7)

Montana Ranger's Wedding Vow (#8)

Montana SEAL Undercover Daddy (#9)

Cape Cod SEAL Rescue (#10)

Montana SEAL Friendly Fire (#11)

Montana SEAL's Mail-Order Bride (#12)

SEAL Justice (#13)

Ranger Creed (#14)

Delta Force Rescue (#15)

Dog Days of Christmas (#16)

Montana Rescue (#17)

Montana Ranger Returns (#18)

As always, with special thanks to Elle James for inviting me into her world of Brotherhood Protectors.

GUARDIAN AGENCY: TYLER

When hope is lost, truth is blurred, and your life is on the line,
it's time to call in the Guardian Agency...

She's a vigilante on a mission... Can a helpful stranger save her from herself?

Autumn Curley has no interest in changing her ways. After escaping her captors, her sole purpose is to destroy the gangs that prey on Native American women and make sure no one else suffers like she did. But she doesn't know the gangs are closing in and about to spring a trap.

A former airman, Tyler Vidro now works as behind-the-scenes support for the Guardian Agency bodyguards. He's been privately searching for Autumn since she disappeared after delivering testimony in an important trial against the violent gangs operating on tribal lands.

After months of analysis, Tyler knows the gangs are determined to stop Autumn—permanently. To save her life, he must step out of his comfort zone and into the field. If he can't earn her trust, she'll never have a chance to truly heal.

Visit ReganBlack.com for a full list of books,
excerpts and upcoming release dates.
For early access to new releases, exclusive prizes,
and much more,
subscribe to Regan's monthly newsletter.

CHAPTER 1

HEADLINE: *Shoplifter Gift-wrapped and Delivered to Tribal Police*

ALONE IN HIS OFFICE, Tyler Vidro laughed softly as he read the brief report from the Blackfeet reservation. A few days ago, someone had caught a shoplifter, hogtied him, and hauled both the offender and the stolen goods to the police station. The young man, listed as nineteen years old, had been deposited at the side of the building and found shivering and furious after a night of hard rain. He'd also been in possession of enough cocaine that authorities were charging him with intent to distribute.

This was her work. Had to be connected to the

woman he was searching for. No one else had this particular combination of dark humor, strong sense of justice, and the ability to pull it off.

He scanned news articles daily as part of his role as an information and technical assistant with the Guardian Agency. The habit kept him sharp and helped him provide background and support for the agency bodyguards on their various cases. He also kept a close eye on petty crimes and mysterious instances of crimes averted near the Native American Indian reservations in and around Montana.

At one time he'd done it as part of a case, now it was solely a personal effort to find one lost needle in a haystack. A needle that refused to come out into the light.

Over a year ago, the law firm of Gamble and Swann, the team that served as the face of the Guardian Agency to shield the identity of its founder, had taken on a high-profile case as a favor to the Federal Prosecutor in Helena, Montana. Three women, all important witnesses in a major kidnapping and human trafficking case, had been flushed out of protective custody. Agency body-guards had been sent to find them and make sure they survived to testify against the accused.

Thanks to the Guardian Agency, and the expert

assistance of the Brotherhood Protectors, another security firm owned and operated by a retired Navy SEAL, everything had worked out for the prosecutor. She got her conviction in that case, as well as solid, actionable intel on a gang that was dealing Native American women and girls like any other illegal commodity.

The victory was huge but the celebration was muted. One witness, the woman who'd escaped her captors after nearly two years and blown the whistle on the previously unnamed leaders of the Native Mob, remained in the wind: Autumn Curley.

The woman who had surely delivered another petty thief to the tribal police.

She had miraculously survived without assistance after her secure location as a witness had been compromised. During the trial, she'd testified from a remote location, moving several members of the jury to tears as she recounted the kidnapping and captivity. She'd given the prosecutor every name and address and pattern she'd memorized along with detailed accounts of dreadful crimes she'd witnessed. And then she'd disappeared.

But Tyler knew better than most that, outside of mystery novels and thrillers, people didn't just vanish. Not with cameras on nearly every street corner and cell phones that were always on and broadcasting to the internet. A person could consciously avoid social media, but any brush with the public was a potential for exposure.

Those random interactions were often Tyler's hunting ground during a case, whether his bodyguard needed a clean escape route or an overview of the habits of a potential perp or victim.

And, unlike most people who were mystified by her disappearance, he had a better understanding of why Autumn didn't want to be found. It was hard to face people, to participate in normal activities or feel any connection after a life-altering event. What she must have seen and survived as a captive in the Native Mob system was unfathomable. Horrific. He couldn't imagine how she was coping with the emotional fallout. Recovering and moving on after a tragic experience was a big challenge even with a dedicated, attentive support team of compassionate family, friends, and professionals. He'd learned that the hard way.

The way Autumn cut herself off from family, friends, and basically the world in general worried him. Her sister, Summer, another witness in the case, had been desperate for a reunion, but when given the opportunity, Autumn had gone into hiding instead.

Tyler wanted to help. Whatever her reasons—shame or guilt or frustration or fear—he felt compelled to reassure her that she wasn't alone. This case wouldn't be closed for him until he knew she was all right. Safe from her trauma and memories and, more importantly, safe from the criminal organization she'd turned inside out.

After every bit of background he'd dug up on the Curley sisters through the course of the initial case, he suspected she stayed away from her dad and sister because she was afraid the gangs seeking vengeance would catch up with her and hurt them both. It might not be the primary reason, but it had to be a factor.

He told himself he couldn't forget Autumn because Summer was now the wife of Colin, a Guardian Agency bodyguard Tyler often assisted. On busy days he almost believed it. But when things were too quiet in his office, or when his mind wandered during his down time, he had to face the truth: he'd become obsessed with finding her.

To that end, despite the official status of the case, he continued to scan the police blotters and obscure local news reports for leads. Whenever possible, he traveled to search an area personally for any sign of her. None of those treks had panned out. Yet. He took full advantage of the liberal Guardian Agency personal leave policy and he refused to give up on his quest.

Remaining isolated after what she'd endured couldn't be healthy and if anyone deserved full restoration and renewed peace, she did.

Several months ago, Colin had asked if Tyler believed Autumn was still alive. Tyler was certain she was, if only because the Native Mob hadn't done any boasting about capturing the woman they considered a mortal enemy to their individual gangs as well as the operation as a whole. More low- and mid-level members of Native American gangs in Montana and the surrounding area had been rounded up in the time since Autumn's disappearance than in the previous two years of her captivity. Tyler didn't think that was a coincidence.

Early in his search, when he failed to find Autumn by normal means, he'd resorted to a tactic they'd used to find the other two witnesses: track the gang's movements and chatter. Although the strategy had paid off and he'd been close, he'd never able to make contact.

He had no way to prove that the anonymous tips and the occasional call to pick up a thief or vandal caught in the act were her work, but who else had the motivation to take those risks? No one condoned the crimes that ranged from petty theft to kidnapping, but no one else was taking a stand in the same way as this ghost-like vigilante.

Tyler had studied the lengthy history and evolution of the gangs that had grown up from the reservations. They weren't the forgiving sort. Autumn had cost them money and stained the organization's reputation. Retaliation wasn't a troubling theory, it was a given.

His current assumption was that she was hiding somewhere on the reservations, but so far he hadn't found any helpful clues in the Curley family past to guide him. The only property of record was the farm where her father still lived and that would've put her dad in harm's way.

He returned to the article, pulled up a map of the area surrounding the station where the shoplifter had been dumped. Unlike the media frenzy that swirled around Autumn's escape and the trial that followed, stories like the shoplifter barely made it to the local media outlets. He suspected the law enforcement offices on the receiving end believed she was behind the random drop-offs too. So far no one had called her by name, she was simply a legend, a ghost who tracked down the bad and the ugly and delivered them for justice.

No one complained about gangbangers getting caught for the petty stuff or serious crimes, they were just happy to take delivery and press charges. He wondered if anyone in the criminal justice system worried as much as he did that eventually Autumn wouldn't be able to outmaneuver the Native Mob as well as she avoided security cameras around the police stations.

The mob would move on her. And soon, if he was reading the current chatter correctly. Dean Mosley was at the top of the food chain among the Native Mob in and around Montana and all signs pointed to his patience running out with Autumn's interference. In the past month she'd trussed up and dropped off this shoplifter, one of Mosley's most trusted managers, and one of his top drivers.

Either she was getting cocky or she was developing an outright death wish.

It was a miracle she wasn't killing everyone she nabbed who was connected to Mosley's trafficking ring, although he suspected she had that in mind for Mosley himself when she found him. Tyler needed to find her before that happened, before she reached the point of no return.

Though her citizen arrests seemed random,

he'd discovered that her drop-offs did coincide with Mosley's movements between reservations and city centers in the area. She tended to attack when he was elsewhere, exploiting the weaknesses of those he left in charge.

The shoplifter had been caught and delivered to authorities on the Blackfeet reservation, so she wouldn't stay in that vicinity for long. She had to have some kind of base that provided good access between the reservations where she was hunting gangbangers. But when he'd crunched the numbers, the pin landed in Helena and though he'd searched via camera feeds and in person he'd never found her where he should have.

Which left him stuck in his office, watching and waiting for a new, viable lead. Doing his homework on the shoplifter, the connection to Mosley popped up quickly and left Tyler reeling. He rubbed his temples. "Damn it, Autumn. You're playing with fire." This time she'd hauled in Mosley's nephew.

Sure enough, when he drilled down across social media, he found a selfie just before the kid committed his crime. The comments on the post confirmed his worst fears that finding Autumn, although she hadn't been named specifically, was now the mob's top priority. A bounty had been posted and Tyler's heart sank when he verified it wasn't just bravado.

Several comments on the post already claimed sightings and tips on the vigilante. He dismissed those in the immediate vicinity of the shoplifting incident and searched those that were closer to known hang outs of gang members in Helena and areas south. Two more specific comments caught his eye, both claiming sightings on the Crow reservation and both from last night. The women who'd posted the comments were inexplicably sure that the female bartender at the bar was somehow involved with the nephew's arrest.

That alone wouldn't have been enough for him to plan another attempt to locate her, but he'd also learned that the smaller gangs were gearing up for some significant event on Crow territory. If he'd heard about it, chances were good Autumn had too and was planning to make a move. He had to get out there.

Would Gamble and Swann give him more time off?

The last time he had tried to work remotely and support one of the Guardian Agency body-guards while searching for Autumn had backfired. He wouldn't take that kind of chance with another case. Fortunately, it had been a relatively straightforward situation, but it would've been resolved more efficiently if Tyler hadn't botched the physical description of the old boyfriend stalking the client.

He could not ignore this. Autumn had survived God only knew what during her captivity. She needed *someone* watching her back if the gangs were closing in on her. What she'd shared with the federal prosecutor had exposed dreadful corruption within the tribal communities and painted a target on her back. The ripples were still pushing out, affecting people, and due to the pervasive influence of Mosley's mob, he wasn't sure anyone on the reservations would help even if she did ask.

He picked up the phone and called the law firm. When the receptionist answered he asked to speak with Swann.

"Tyler," Swann answered. "What can I do for you?" He didn't sound eager, which Tyler deserved after pushing the limits of the agency's patience.

"I need to ask—"

"You'd best not end that sentence with the word vacation," Swann warned.

Tyler cringed. "Then I guess we need to negotiate a leave of absence." He didn't really want to sacrifice the best job he'd had since leaving the military.

"Are you serious?" Swann demanded. Tyler could picture him leaning into the phone, his tailored suit working overtime to contain his frustration. "Son, we have gone above and beyond to accommodate you. You keep telling me it's not a medical concern, but it's clearly personal. If you're not dying, who is?"

"Sir." Tyler wanted to be honest, he just didn't know how to do that without exposing Autumn to a search that could get her killed. "This past year has been difficult and I appreciate the grace you've given me. If I need to resign—"

"No." Swann cut him off again. "Let me shuffle things around. You currently don't have any active cases?"

"That's right," Tyler confirmed.

"How much time do you think you'll need?"

Tough to say. In the past he'd limited himself to three or four days to search. The bodyguards weren't locked into a standard work week because protecting people was a twenty-four/seven deal. They did however cycle cases to give people time off between cases to reduce the risk of burnout.

"One week should be—will be—enough," Tyler said. Though he hated setting the limit, he needed it, both as a man and as an employee. If he couldn't track down Autumn this time, he'd have to accept defeat on this case.

Swann was quiet for so long Tyler double-checked that the line was still open and the call hadn't dropped. "Do you expect to need backup?" he finally asked.

"No, sir," Tyler replied. This would be so much easier if he had the confidence to explain it all. But he wasn't an investigator, not like the bodyguards in the field and as far as the agency was concerned, this case was over and done.

"I'm not happy accepting your excuse that this is another personal matter," Swann said.

"I understand." The warning was clear, as was the invitation to open up. He was working for an investigations agency. With the resources at their fingertips, the odds were good that Swann already knew what had consumed him recently. He hadn't spotted a tail, but it was possible he'd missed something that would've been obvious to one of the bodyguards.

"It has become personal," he began. "Though it started with a case that was brought to us."

Swann swore. "You're tracking that lost witness."

"Yes, sir," Tyler replied, though it hadn't been a question. Communications had been compromised during the active case. He prayed Swann wouldn't say her name over the phone.

"You've been handling all of this on your personal time because?"

Tyler was stumped. It hadn't occurred to him to ask the agency to join the search for Autumn. She was a cold case. They'd fulfilled the obligation to the prosecutor. The Guardian Agency worked to prevent immediate and *present* threats to their clients. Aside from her sister, Tyler had assumed he was the only person interested in finding her.

Not even her father had expressed much concern over his younger daughter's status as missing. For a time Tyler thought that was because he was helping her hide from the Native Mob, but his theory had been blown out of the water when she'd started leaving criminals on law enforcement doorsteps.

Swann cleared his throat. "I'm waiting."

"Because it feels personal," Tyler answered. "I never knew her personally, but as we dug into the case for the prosecutor, something about her clicked with me." He hoped that would suffice because he didn't have a better reasoning.

"She's your white whale kind of mission?"

"I guess that's accurate," Tyler agreed.

"All right, take your time and be careful out

there. Now that you've confirmed what you're up against, I will have someone close in case you get in over your head."

"Thank you, sir. For what it's worth, I'd planned to reach out to Hank Patterson's Brotherhood Protectors."

"Not a bad choice," Swann allowed. "You've made good friends in Montana?"

Even that felt like too much information to confirm or deny over an open phone line. Mosley's crew had proved their long reach when they'd nearly succeeded in sidelining the original case. "Mostly because of location and their quick response time."

"There is that," Swann agreed. "No one mobilizes quite like a former SEAL."

"True." Tyler had served as an Air Force analyst, but taking offense wouldn't help him here.

"Let me reach out," he said. "You just focus on what you need to do. Keep me in the loop this time."

Swann ended the call before Tyler could argue over the wisdom of sharing who he found, when, and where.

He packed up quickly, starting with the tools that served his strengths: laptop, cell phone, and a signal booster for those places where cell coverage was scarce. He threw in clothes that would tolerate the rugged conditions and packed his tactical knife, his handgun, and ammunition.

He was well aware Autumn did not want to be found. But someone had to warn her that her enemies were more determined than ever and closing in.

CHAPTER 2

ON A CLEAR AND balmy spring evening, Hank Patterson walked with his wife, Sadie, under a pastel-painted sky. Snow lingered on the Crazy Mountains, bright highlights gleaming with the last rays of sunlight.

"Think we'll get more snow before spring takes hold for good?" Sadie asked, linking her hand with his.

"It's Montana," he reminded her with a wink. This time they took, just the two of them, had become one of his favorite hours of every day. A chance to chat and reconnect with the person who mattered most to his heart and soul.

"Nikki called earlier," she said. "She and Brett are back in Charleston and she sounds more content than I've ever heard her."

He slipped his arm around her waist. "Never underestimate the power of true love."

"Is that your secret super power?" she teased.

He pulled her close for a quick kiss. He would never get enough of her. "Absolutely."

As they continued their walk, he thought about how much could change in a year. "I'm glad she's happy," he said. "Brett's a good man." They'd met the former SEAL, now with the Guardian Agency, when Sadie's friend Nikki had needed protection from a stalker.

"He is, but he is second to one man in particular." Sadie gave Hank a little hip bump.

His cell phone vibrated in his back pocket and he wagged his eyebrows. "You've got some skills," he joked as he checked the caller ID. "Huh. It's Claudia," he said before he answered.

Claudia had been with the CIA and they'd met during Hank's career as a Navy SEAL. She currently used her research, analysis, and technical skills to support bodyguards like Brett with the Guardian Agency. Hank regretted that he hadn't known when she left government service. She would've been a huge asset to his company.

With a nod, Sadie walked on ahead giving him some space to speak privately.

He appreciated his wife's discretion in business

matters though there really weren't any secrets between them. "Hi, Claudia."

"Hank." She sounded relieved. "I hope I didn't catch you at a bad time."

"You're interrupting a stunning sunset, but I can spare a few minutes."

"Thanks," she replied with a smile in her voice. "I've got a potential situation brewing."

"Usually the case in our line of work."

"Tell me about it. Do you remember Tyler?"

"Sure." Like Claudia, Tyler supported bodyguards for their security agency from behind the scenes. And he had done a tremendous job when things turned ugly with a federal case against the Native Mob being tried in Helena.

"I believe he's in your neck of the woods," she said. "My bosses would consider it a personal favor if you would keep an eye out for him."

"That's just ambiguous enough to hold my interest," Hank said. "What are you really asking for?"

She sighed. "I wish I knew. Tyler has taken a lot of time off in the last year. I don't have all the details, but it's likely that whatever he's working on will turn dangerous."

Brotherhood Protectors and the Guardian Agency had been cooperating with great success since that case went sideways in Helena. "If I'm hearing you right, you want me on standby."

"Yes, please. And thank you. As soon as I get any helpful details I'll send them on. I was told he planned to reach out to you if things got sticky."

"Haven't heard from him yet, so I appreciate the warning. Guess bodyguards are like real estate, location, location, location," he said, trying to lighten the mood. Claudia rarely exhibited stress, but he knew her well.

They chatted for a minute about family things and then wrapped up the call. Breaking into a jog, he caught up with Sadie.

"Everything all right?" she asked.

"Seems to be. Sounds like one of her people is in our area," he replied.

"But nothing urgent?"

"Not yet." He smiled. "If it gets that way—"

She turned to wrap her arms around his waist. "If it goes any kind of way you'll handle it like you always do," she finished for him.

He bent his head and kissed her smiling lips. There, with the twilight sky overhead, his land under his feet and his wife in his arms, Hank was swamped with a love, peace, and contentment he'd never expected and would never take for granted.

CHAPTER 3

AUTUMN CURLEY WENT by Amber Cree here in the rural town a few miles off the main highway that bisected the Crow Reservation. She held down two jobs, first as a bartender at the dive on the rough side of Main Street and also as a housekeeper at the motel. One gave her a good cash flow, the other a safe place to stay.

Both jobs gave her plenty of access to the gossip mill, such as it was, in a town of a thousand or so permanent residents as well as news shared by people, usually truckers, passing through.

For several months now, this had been more or less a permanent home base. A place to recuperate while she kept her ear to the ground about gang activity in the area. The Native Mob had the local gangs under control and the overarching enterprise was insidious. Everyone knew the gangs ran drugs and guns, but they pumped just enough of that blood money back to people and businesses on the reservation to stay out of jail.

Good people who would be appalled to learn the mob was stealing Native American girls and women and selling them into the sex trade and slavery, chose to stay quiet about the more common crimes.

Autumn was quiet about the gang activity, but for different reasons. She'd been inside the twisted heart of the mob, had the scars on her body and soul to prove it. Although she couldn't state her true feelings without revealing her real identity, she was done pretending there was anything benevolent about the gangs at any level of the operation.

It had taken time to find this town, a place where she could work and listen and be invisible to the residents and those passing through. She used snippets of conversations, news reports, and her experiences as the mob's captive to interfere in gang business. Focused mainly on the small-time offenders, she'd been working her way up the chain of command. Soon she'd have Mosley, reigning king of the mob, under her knife.

Word was circulating in dark corners that

Mosely would soon return to the Crow reservation for a complex strategy session or to finalize a big deal. Not guns or drugs, his lieutenants could handle those deals. If he was on hand, she was sure the deal involved his biggest profit margin: human trafficking.

Behind the curtain, she'd learned that the gangs considered the girls of their tribes a free and therefore disposable commodity. It rarely cost more than a tank of gas to pluck a girl right out of her life. A few inexpensive doses of heroin later and the girls were pliable and ready to sell. Inside, it had been a misery to watch those girls and young women give up, the fire in their eyes extinguished by constant abuse. The girls she'd been inside with had called her lucky when Mosley stopped dosing her. She would never understand his decision and she had too much compassion to tell them how terrible it was to have a clear view while they were being slowly killed.

She would never forget those hopeless, bleak days, but taking action, even if it was only pestering local gang members, helped her feel as if she was making progress while she waited for the right moment to strike Mosley directly.

Today, as she cleaned the recently vacated rooms, her heavy dark hair was pulled up into a top knot and covered with a baseball cap that had been left behind by a motel guest. Most of the time she used colored hair pieces or a full blonde wig as a disguise in public, but the wig was hot and itchy when she worked up a sweat.

Just over an hour later, she was rolling her housekeeping cart back toward the storage area behind the central office when she sensed trouble. It was too soon for official guest check-ins, though all the rooms were clean. From her vantage point she could watch the parking lot without being obvious. A silver-blue pickup truck with Wyoming plates had stopped in front of the office. The man who emerged was too clean-cut and freshly scrubbed to be a local. His beard was perfectly trim, his jacket and boots weren't even dusty. Sunshine highlighted the gold strands in his gleaming brown hair. He wasn't bulky, but he had a swagger that implied he could handle himself. She caught herself wondering what color his eyes were behind the sunglasses. No. She didn't need to get that close to anyone. Not ever again.

She had the strange feeling she'd seen him before. Usually when that happened, her shoulders tensed and her body prepared to flee. The people she met most often these days were outright crimi-nals or blurring the edge of legal at the very least.

This time, her first impression didn't make her feel ill-at-ease. She watched him until he disappeared into the office. Maybe he was a reporter and she'd seen that handsome face on the news.

That didn't quite fit though. During her time as a prisoner, she'd learned to read people as a mode of survival, from the guards who watched their every move to the clients who examined them like produce on display at a market. She hadn't run into this man in those venues.

He exited the office and walked down the sidewalk, passing right by without seeing her. She was used to being invisible, preferred it actually, after so many months being paraded about. At his room he double checked the number on the key and the door, then glanced around before he entered. Demonstrating caution was a good thing, especially when he stood out the way he did. He carried a little too much city polish to really fit in around here.

She would have to keep an eye on him if he stayed more than one night. Might even snoop through his room for insight into his purpose here. Odds were low his arrival had anything to do with her, but something about that familiar sensation wouldn't let her dismiss him outright.

She didn't need any extra surprises when she was this close to her goal.

Once she was sure he wasn't coming back out, she went into the office and turned in her master keys. "Everything is clean and good to go," she reported.

"Thanks, Amber," Debbie replied.

Debbie and her husband Jeff owned the motel and Autumn counted them among the few good people she knew. They didn't ask too many questions and they didn't judge her odd habits or absences. Debbie provided excellent customer service and Jeff handled the repairs and maintenance and landscaping.

Autumn wasn't sure what motivated the couple to stick it out here, with a business that barely scraped by, but she was thankful for them. She'd counted it a stroke of tremendous good luck when she had been able to bargain for a room in exchange for the housekeeping services. The property was small but Debbie and Jeff clearly took pride in it.

Since coming here and finding some routine, Autumn had experienced strange flashes of being normal. Like a memory that was fuzzy around the edges, but made her feel good.

"The new guy looks sort of fancy," she said.

"A little." Debbie fluffed her pewter hair. "I think he's former military."

"Did he ask for a discount?"

"No, nothing like that." Debbie waved off such an obvious clue. "Just the way he carried himself. Y'know, like he was used to good posture and staying alert."

Autumn chuckled. She was used to staying alert and she'd never spent a day in any place as organized and regimented as the military. "Seems a little young for military if you ask me."

"I guess so." Debbie clucked her tongue. "But not everyone gives thirty years anymore."

She had a point. "So he's passing through or here to stay?"

"Why are you so curious?" Debbie wondered.

Autumn shrugged. "Just call me bored."

"You can quiz him all you want down at the bar tonight."

That earned Autumn's full attention. "He mentioned the bar?" Was Mr. Clean-cut a new player in Mosley's games?

"Not specifically," Debbie said. "Where else is he going to go? They have the coldest beer in town."

"Not if you'd add mini-fridges to the rooms."

"As if," Debbie said with a laugh.

The happy sound never ceased to lift Autumn's heart. "He didn't strike me as the type to go looking for trouble."

"All men that age are looking for trouble in one form or another," Debbie countered, a knowing gleam in her eyes.

In Autumn's experience, men who *did* look for trouble didn't age out of those tendencies, but it wasn't worth an argument. "The linens are in the wash," she said changing the subject. "I'll be back around to move them to the dryer. Do you need me to take care of anything else?"

"Can't think of a thing. Sounds like you've got it all covered, honey. Thank you."

Autumn returned to her room, going the back way just to avoid bumping into the new guest. She'd hoped to find his name on the register, but a smooth and reasonable way behind the counter hadn't presented itself. For the first time in ages, she wished for a computer. The cell phone she used was outdated by several generations. She could use the device for online access, but it was slow and the screen was small and cracked.

She *knew* that man's face and she didn't believe in coincidences. Falling back on the bed, she stared up at the ceiling, yellowed from previous guests who ignored the no-smoking rule. Her door was locked and the curtains drawn, so she closed her eyes, determined to put that face into context. Determined to remember him.

He had confidence without any of the mean edges of the clients Mosley brought to the auctions and parties. Her intuition wanted to fit him into her original protective detail, but that wasn't it either. Maybe he'd been at the courthouse, working in some capacity during the course of her trial.

What she feared most was that he was connected to the prosecutor's office. Someone there had been bought off by the Native Mob. Autumn hadn't stuck around long enough to learn the name of the person who had been turned against the justice system, sharing confidential information with the gang leaders.

Since she'd started dropping the small fish within the gangs on police station doorsteps, reporters would periodically show up in search of the mysterious vigilante. So far no one had connected her with any of those events. She'd even given a comment to one reporter a few months back, praising the vigilante's efforts. In learning to read people, she'd also learned how to present herself to serve her purposes. Meek when she needed to be, bold when she was in disguise.

Debbie and Jeff saw a young woman down on her luck who needed some time and space to get herself together. They thought she was nice and caring and hard-working. Only one of those descriptors was true. She didn't mind hard work, never had. Nice and caring? She wasn't sure she had that in her anymore.

Down at the bar, the customers interacted with an aloof, confident woman with pessimistic tendencies. Oh, she listened in the bartender tradition, but she only offered another drink, not advice or opinions.

The alarm on her phone chimed, pulling her out of her reverie. Time to move the laundry from washer to dryer. After nearly an hour thinking about it, she was no closer to figuring out where she'd seen the new guest before. Well, eventually it would come to her. At that point she could decide how to proceed.

For now, she needed to psych herself up for her shift at the bar tonight. If she could get a few locals primed and talkative, she could move a step closer to finding and destroying Mosley.

CHAPTER 4

IN THE MOTEL ROOM, Tyler dropped his duffel on the bed and carefully unpacked his computer from his backpack. Keeping Swann informed, he used his cell phone to text a message with his location. To his shock a reply came back immediately.

Claudia is your support contact.

Oh, man. Tyler swore. Swann was behaving as if Tyler was now an agency protector. Maybe he had changed roles, but not officially. Definitely not permanently. He wouldn't need tech support for this if he could find Autumn and convince her to stop pestering the gangs. His primary goal was to turn this cold case into case closed and make sure all parties were safe.

There was one glaring reason Swann had put Claudia on alert that Tyler couldn't ignore. She had the best connection to Patterson's security company. The Brotherhood Protectors were likely the fastest response if he did get into serious trouble out here. Protesting backup of any kind was a dumb move. There was no way to know how Autumn would react and he didn't want to lose track of her again.

His gaze shifted between his computer and the door. The lock wasn't exactly state-of-the-art and that chain wouldn't put up much of a resistance if tested. Probably best to keep his belongings with him or hidden. The motel was the only option in this miniscule town, unless he chose to rough it out at a campsite.

Once his laptop was up to speed, he checked his cloud service, skimming through the notes he'd uploaded after his chat with the tribal police on the Blackfeet reservation. The teenager who had been dumped on their doorstep didn't have a reputation beyond being Mosley's nephew. No one had been surprised when he'd dropped out of high school for gang life, but so far he hadn't made much of a splash. He was a low-level dealer who did a little bit of everything as ordered.

They police had shared the videos from all their cameras and he didn't find anything they'd overlooked. How did Autumn navigate without being seen? In her place, he might've relied on signal jammers, a mask to hide his face, or gone old school and blocked the camera lens. There were risks to each approach, but those risks seemed like better alternatives to getting caught.

She hadn't done any of those things and remained invisible.

Despite the lack of proof, he felt as though he was making progress. Last night, he'd reviewed hours of available traffic camera footage following the drop off, looking for any sign of Autumn behind the wheel.

He believed in and trusted gut instinct although he had more faith in his own intuition behind a computer than out in the field. Still, when he'd caught sight of a weathered, charcoal gray hatchback at several points on the most direct route across Montana, he'd perked up. The driver's face had been obscured by a baseball cap with a logo for a regional minor league team and could've belonged to a teenage boy or a young woman, but Tyler suspected it was her.

He'd lost the vehicle moving south on the highway, not long after it crossed into the Crow Reservation. It made sense to him that Autumn would have her own methods for keeping tabs on the gang and she had probably heard Mosley was visiting this area too.

Yes, he could call Swann and ask for a real protector to be assigned to her case. And doing so put everything he'd worked for at risk. Every detail he'd mined from Summer about her sister and matched up with the vigilante's actions told him Autumn would bolt if a stranger showed up claiming to help her.

Not that she knew him, but he was confident he understood her. He knew how she processed information, how she thought, and how she took action. Right now those details were more impor-tant than knowing her favorite color, where she was working, and how she managed to stay off the grid.

Since this case had landed with the Guardian Agency, he'd studied the pictures provided by law enforcement and her sister. He'd reviewed her school records and her hobbies before she'd been abducted. Through conversations with Summer, he'd learned Autumn had hoped for a career in the National Parks Service.

Instead, she'd turned into a lone warrior fighting a massive criminal organization.

Doing his best to behave like the bodyguards he

assisted, he called Claudia. "Did you find that gray hatchback?" he asked as soon as she answered.

"No." She sighed. "I've searched everywhere, Ty."

"All right. It's possible she's camping somewhere on the reservation or in one of the national parks nearby."

"Possible? That's closer to a ninety-eight percent certainty. How else would she go this long without being caught or noticed?"

"How small is that town you and Nathan are living in?"

"Microscopic some days," she admitted. "But I checked your location when you stopped. You're in a much smaller town than I am, which only proves my theory. Autumn would've been noticed there. Her face was all over the news in the days following the conviction. Someone would've spotted her, reported her to the gangs or the authorities."

"True. But that car wasn't designed for off-roading." The decision to broadcast her picture, to ask for help from the public had struck him as highly irresponsible at the time. For several weeks he was sure the tactic had gotten her killed.

"I agree," Claudia continued. "I've followed the

cameras on routes to camping areas, but no luck. Your girl might as well be vapor."

"Did you pick up anything new about Mosley's movements?" he asked.

"Nothing you don't already know," Claudia reported. "If he isn't already on Crow land, he will be soon."

He heard that as more confirmation that Autumn must also be somewhere close. Mosley was notorious for his expectations of loyalty and his heavy-handed punishments when someone stepped out of line. Tyler expected Mosley's plans for Autumn to be humiliating and violent before he killed her to make his point.

"One more thing," Claudia said, interrupting his dark thoughts. "I called a friend in the FBI for information on trafficking. Their sources caught wind of an order for a fresh, natural girl."

A chill slid down Tyler's spine. "Haven't heard that one before."

"Me neither. Add it to the things I wish I'd never learned. My contact says fresh usually means virgin. Looking at the notes from the case, Autumn stated that Mosley would often fulfill specific orders for clients."

"I remember." That code couldn't refer to Autumn, not after nearly two years inside

Mosley's system. If 'natural' was a code for Native American, it was more likely Mosley meant to kidnap a new girl while he was in the area.

"Is there any way to put out an alert without tipping off the mob?" he asked.

"Probably not, but I already did it," she admitted, her voice rough with emotion. "This crew is pure arrogance. They think they're untouchable. I'm sure they'll take action even if they hear the authorities are expecting something."

"It's a big territory," he said, studying the map he'd pulled up online.

"Do you want some help covering it?"

He would've been offended if he hadn't asked that same question time and again while supporting other bodyguards. "Not yet. Too many strangers could spook her or the gangs."

"All right," she said. "Just remember help is one text message away."

"Thanks. That means a lot." He shut everything down when the call finished. Shrugging into his shoulder holster, he checked his gun, secured it, and then slipped into his denim jacket. Grabbing his cell phone and his keys, he went to his truck to familiarize himself with the town.

Of course he was also looking for the gray

hatchback, or anyone wearing a baseball cap similar to what he'd seen on the driver.

He had to accept the possibility that she was camping out in the wilderness where he'd never find her. The gray hatchback might be nothing more than a random vehicle he'd fixated on by mistake. No, he didn't have much confidence in his field skills, but he couldn't give up.

Main Street was a straight division through the town and the anchoring businesses extended for a little over a mile of clean, well-kept store fronts. No need for a traffic light, just a four way stop at the central intersection. Whoever carved this town out of the tough Montana terrain had been deliberate about it. Turning, he aimed back toward the motel, driving one block off of Main. The further he traveled from the center of town, the rougher the profile of the buildings. There were a few boarded up windows and closed businesses peppered with places trying to stay viable.

It seemed like the motel and a glossy new truck stop anchored the north end of town, closest to the highway access, while a grimy bar with plenty of neon and a grocery store that had seen better days held down the south end of town. To the west, faded clapboard houses were lined up in neat rows, but most were in some state of decay. Cars and smaller pickup trucks were wedged into skinny driveways or lining the curbs, whittling a two-lane street down to one lane.

Though he cruised through every inch of paved road in and around town, he had yet to spot the gray hatchback. It would be humiliating to admit defeat, even if Swann or Claudia or anyone else understood why he couldn't stop searching for Autumn.

He had six days of his week left. How could he increase the odds of success out here? With the town mapped out in his head, he stopped to fill up the truck and grab a sandwich at the truck stop before returning to the motel across the street.

While he waited for his food, a gray hatchback rolled up to one of the gas pumps. The plate matched the car he and Claudia had been tracking. He held his breath, letting it out in a rush of disappointment when a slender blonde woman emerged from the driver's seat.

Not Autumn.

Based on the snug jeans clinging to her lean legs and the cropped top that hinted at a toned midriff, he thought she was about the right age. Maybe Autumn had borrowed the car from a friend or maybe this woman had borrowed the car from Autumn.

He started for the door, turning back when his name was called to pick up his food. That was all the time necessary for the blonde to drive away.

He cussed himself out for missing a golden opportunity to find a lead. Until he caught a glimpse of the same gray hatchback parked behind the motel. He returned to his room and dropped off his sandwich and then jogged around for a closer look. Making a mental note of the nearby room numbers, he walked through the breezeway to the front office.

The friendly woman who'd checked him in came out when the front door chimed. "Hello again," she said with a smile. "How can I help?"

He glanced at her nametag. "This is an unorthodox question, Debbie, but can you tell me anything about the woman with the gray hatchback?" He gave the license plate number and room numbers near the car.

Debbie's smile faltered and warm gaze cooled. "I'm afraid not. We honor the expectation of guest privacy here."

"And, as a guest, I appreciate it," Tyler said, scrambling now. "I don't mean any harm. In fact I work for a security company and we've been tracking that car to locate and warn a person who might be in danger."

"Is that so?"

"It is." He handed her an agency business card. "Call, check my story. I just need to ask her a few questions."

Debbie flicked his business card with a fingernail. "Write down your questions I'll pass them along."

"So you know her."

"I didn't say that."

She didn't have to. "When is she expected to check out?"

"Mr. Vidro, I will not release details about one guest to another."

"Not even if it's a matter of life and death?"

Debbie pursed her lips. "Far as I'm concerned *you* are the only threat I see. A threat to my sanity and a threat to guest privacy. If you want to stay in my motel, you'll behave yourself and refrain from harassing other travelers."

"All right." He raised his hands in surrender. "I respect your integrity." He did, though it was damned annoying in the moment. Asking permission with a glance, and waiting for Debbie's approval, he picked up a pen from the registration counter and looked around for a notepad.

With a gusty sigh, she handed him a pad of

paper with the motel logo at the top as well as an envelope.

Tyler dashed off a quick note explaining his role as a Guardian Agency investigator. It was only a small stretch of the facts and it gave Autumn reason to trust him, assuming she recognized the company name. He added his request to ask her a few questions regarding a sensitive case.

Debbie didn't even pretend to give him privacy and when she bit her lip he was sure she could read upside down with perfect comprehension. He quickly wrote a copy of the note to leave at the gray hatchback and sealed both notes into envelopes.

"If you have any information—"

She shook her head. "Your business is not my business." She took the first envelope from him.

"Thank you for delivering that for me."

"And where are you going with that one?"

He arched an eyebrow, pausing just long enough to make it obvious he found the query intrusive. "I'll leave it at the car that caught my attention," he replied.

"I see." She tapped the envelope to the registration book. "You don't trust me?"

That wasn't precisely his concern. "You seem quite protective of your, ah, guest. As I said, I respect that. But the information I have is quite urgent and I don't want to take any chances."

Debbie gave a short, decisive nod, though Tyler wasn't sure what sort of decision she'd reached.

"Thanks," he said, starting for the door.

"If you're looking for a place to be other than your motel room, there's a bar at the other end of Main. They have a live band tonight."

"The Wild Bee Tavern?"

"That's the one."

"I'll check it out." Was she giving him some kind of tip or was she hoping to have a window of opportunity to search his room? Only time would tell. He walked back to his room, his rumbling stomach reminding him he'd had a plan before he'd spotted the car.

If that was Autumn's car, she must be working somewhere to raise the cash for gas and maintenance. He wouldn't be surprised if any number of the businesses in town were willing to pay her cash, off the books. That kind of work would explain how she'd survived this long, able to come and go as she pleased, without leaving a typical paper trail.

CHAPTER 5

A<small>UTUMN</small> <small>WATCHED</small> the reactions ripple through the crowd when people noticed the arrival of Jerry King, current top dog of the local gang. His official address was at the west edge of town, where he crashed with his girlfriend and enforcers. The place didn't look like much, but that's because Jerry didn't flaunt the money he stashed under the floor from the drug and gun deals.

Everyone fawned over him, convinced he held some influence with Mosley. She understood the hierarchy, but couldn't explain how little King mattered without exposing herself. Reporting to the boss wasn't the same as being able to sway the boss.

His girlfriend, Cici, had arrived an hour ago with friends in tow to dance and drink. She dashed up to him, her smile dialed up to blinding and her boobs testing the strength of her low cut tee.

As usual, their intimate kiss curdled Autumn's blood.

During her captivity, she'd seen Jerry when he reported to Mosley and she'd watched bruises swell on the girls he chose to use for an hour or two during his visits. Apparently he saved the rough stuff for the disposable girls, since Cici always showed plenty of skin and never a hint of a bruise.

The local power couple sidled up to the bar. "Amber," Jerry called out as if he owned the place. "Set up the whiskey." He held up four fingers.

"Sure thing," she replied. Those two words were her reply to just about everyone. From her first shift, she promised herself she'd treat every customer with the same aloof approach. It made her invisible and gave her a chance to learn so much more. Here, she wasn't a former victim or a mob whistleblower, she was a forgettable bartender without a past who didn't overreact to leering gazes, chauvinist comments, or inadvertent contact.

She set up four shot glasses in front of Jerry and filled them with the best whiskey the bar offered. "On your tab?"

He nodded and tossed back the first shot. Handing the second to Cici, he picked up the third shot in the row. They gave a tiny little clink of their glasses and tipped back their heads in unison.

"We're celebrating," he said, pointing to the last shot. "Join us."

With a vague smile she moved down the bar, checking on customers.

"Come on," Jerry's voice carried over the pulse of the music. "Don't be like that."

She suppressed the shudder at his coaxing tone. As the bartender she was above all this, able to let it roll off without any effect.

He extricated himself from his girlfriend and brought the shot along with him as he followed her down the length of the bar. "I said, take the shot."

"No, thanks." She met his gaze over the taps while she filled a pitcher for the waitress working the pool room. "You enjoy it."

"Hey." He stretched close, his smile slick and oily. "I've got a golden opportunity for you," he said. "Just show me you can play along."

"Can't play while I'm working." She gave the pitcher of beer to the waitress and then scanned the bar for the next customer.

"What if you got paid to drink *and* work?" He

46

pushed the small glass back across the bar, heedless of the whiskey sloshing over the rim. "There's a private event coming up. We could use you. It'll be a prime gig with an open bar."

That kind of private event almost certainly involved Mosley. It was tempting, but she couldn't say yes until she knew for sure. "No thanks."

"Come on," Jerry said. "Five hundred bucks for a couple hours. Plus tips. Everyone important will be there. Just take the shot. Show me you're game."

What was this, middle school peer pressure? His intimidation tactics should've improved with age and experience. She swapped three longnecks for cash and kept moving. "Can't do that. I'm on the clock."

"We've been through this, Amber," Jerry said, his tone menacingly sweet. "What I say trumps your boss."

Hardly. Why did he have to push her tonight when she was already edgy about the stranger at the motel? She hadn't planned on a direct invite to the snake pit—wasn't prepared for that opportunity. Worse, Jerry's persistence was causing a scene and no one would utter a negative word about the gangs around her again if they thought she was connected.

She scooped up a tip as one of her regulars

from the feed store made himself scarce. Jerry had that effect on people, making them scatter. One day soon, she would rile him up and take him down, but not today.

Crooking her finger, she invited him closer. Cici tugged his belt, trying to draw his attention. She failed. Hopefully Autumn's smile was an effective mask for the disgust she felt toward him and all the crimes and trouble he represented. "A word of advice? A tipsy bartender makes costly mistakes." She needed to get him out of the way. The band was wrapping up their second set and she would soon be slammed. "You can buy me a shot when I'm off the clock."

"Now," he insisted. "Do it." He pushed the small glass across the bar with his grease-stained fingertip.

"Sure thing." She accepted the shot glass. "What sort of celebration needs an open bar? You getting married?"

Jerry snorted. "Hell no." He ignored his girlfriend's indignation. "My best friend's in town," he said. The words rang out just as the song ended.

For a split-second the bar went silent. Everyone was aware that Jerry's 'best friend' was Mosley. "We're going fishing. Getting into nature." He sniggered. "Then the party."

Her stomach twisted and tears pricked the back of her eyes. Amber wasn't supposed to have any idea that fishing meant Mosley was in the market for new girls. Jerry had just handed her an engraved invitation to take out the Native Mob leader. It was the opportunity she'd been working for. She wanted to say yes. To down that whiskey and get the date, time and an address right now. But fooling Jerry with a bar between them and the Amber disguise was one thing. A blond wig wouldn't fool Mosley. He'd kept her too close for too long.

"Hooray for you." She lifted the shot high in salute and poured it out over the sink behind the bar. "I hope you all have a grand time."

Jerry turned red and with surprising speed he lunged across the bar. "You bitch!"

Autumn sidestepped his attempt to grab her and returned to the job she'd been hired to do. But customers were being shoved aside and barstools were clattering to the floor in Jerry's wild attempt to get to the pass-through. To get to her.

Let him come. She was primed for a fight, ready to wreck his fishing plans. Her fingers curled around the long neck of a heavy bottle. From the corner of her eye, she noticed Ezra, cook and owner of the bar, at the kitchen door. His presence snapped her back. This wasn't the place to show her real self. Too much attention, too much risk to innocent people and property.

"Ease up, man." One last customer blocked Jerry's path. The new guest at the motel. He didn't dart out of the way when Jerry grabbed him. In fact, the man kept his seat when Jerry gave him a shove. "Take your problem somewhere else."

A collective gasp rippled through the bar.

"The rest of us are here for the music," he added.

"You got it wrong." Jerry squared off with the stranger. "*I* say who does what here."

The clean-cut stranger looked at her. "Is he the owner?"

"No." Autumn snapped, her gaze drifting toward the kitchen door. Ezra just arched an eyebrow, watching carefully.

"Then he can calm down or get out."

Who was this guy to have a spine of steel in the face of a menace like Jerry? Behind her, Ezra chuckled. More nervous laughter bubbled over the gathered crowd.

But Jerry wasn't done. He hauled the man upright and shoved him back against the bar. Autumn recognized that the stranger had allowed it, but Jerry was too full of himself to notice.

He raised his fist to throw a punch but the stranger moved first. Jerry's arm dropped to his side, his eyes watering and his face pale. He couldn't seem to make any sound. Maybe this guy *was* former military.

"Get him out of here," the stranger said, aiming a limp Jerry toward Cici.

The locals, braced for a fight, were baffled when Jerry shuffled away, defeated before any punches had been thrown.

At some signal from Ezra, the band started up with a new song. She'd have to send up fresh water and beer to get them through without a real break.

Autumn eyed the stranger as he resumed his seat and set a fresh pint in front of him. "Lager, right?"

"Right," he said.

"What's a girl gotta do to learn that move?"

The stranger's eyebrows lifted and his eyes—blue, she noticed—held a glint of amusement. "Wouldn't do you much good from that side of the bar."

"I'm not always on this side of the bar," she pointed out.

"In that case…" His voice trailed off as if he was weighing his options. Or maybe his obligations. "I can show you when you're off the clock."

"That's hours yet," she said.

"No problem," he replied. "Beer's cold, music's good, and the company just got a lot better."

Was he referring to her attention or Jerry's exit? Either way, she wanted to learn how he'd ended the fight so quickly. How many times had a man raised a hand to her while she'd been Mosley's property? She stuck out her hand. "I'm Amber."

He matched the gesture. "Tyler."

"How long are you in town, Tyler?"

"As long as it takes."

She had to let that cryptic statement lie as a waitress came over and called out the drinks she needed. But his words echoed in her head for the rest of the night.

TYLER WATCHED the bartender as closely as he dared. The blond wig and skillful makeup didn't match the physical description of Autumn, but he was increasingly certain Amber and Autumn were the same woman.

Did Jerry, leader of the local gang, also realize the pretty bartender he couldn't intimidate was the same person who'd been harassing the gangs? The man hadn't struck him as that perceptive. And

Tyler had to admit, if he'd been in the market for a private bartender, she'd be a good choice. Efficient without being too aloof. Friendly without getting bogged down. She listened to far more than the drink orders shouted at her over the high-volume band.

She wandered back his way to clear the plate of loaded potato bites he'd demolished in the past half hour. "Food's better than I expected," he said.

"Ezra is all about excellent bar food." She shrugged. "Another pint?"

"No thanks. I'm teaching a self-defense lesson in a bit." Her lips tilted up at one side. Was that a rusty attempt at a sincere smile?

Watching her, he'd seen the wariness behind the friendly expressions she gave her customers. This woman was constantly on alert and completely dialed in to her environment. No doubt in his mind it was a result of her ordeal. It was remarkable that she could cope, really. Then again, she'd proven herself a survivor.

A survivor with a mission for justice. He could get behind that, as long as she didn't get hurt again in the process.

Once more he wondered if Jerry had seen through the disguise. Hiring her for a private event would make it easier to trap or kill her. Had she refused because she'd seen through the ploy or because she didn't want to get tangled up with mob business?

Hopefully he would soon have a chance to ask her directly. When the bar closed, he sipped water while the band packed their gear and the staff cleaned up the remnants of a busy night.

"Need a hand?" he asked.

"We've got a system," she said. She counted her drawer and filled a bank bag with the cash. "Sit tight." She disappeared into the kitchen and he caught himself admiring the view as she walked away.

She was a client—probably—and even if she wasn't, she'd asked for a self-defense tip. He didn't need to blur that lesson with a creepy stranger vibe. The goal was to confirm her identity and gain her trust so she would believe him when he explained the mob was closing in on her.

When she came back out to the bar, the cook and two waitresses were with her. After she made introductions, she asked, "Can you show all of us that move?"

"Absolutely." He was grateful to have another man to help him demonstrate. "It's not a hard maneuver, but you have to be quick. And fair warning, it's not always as effective as it was tonight."

He showed them where to strike and how to strike for the best effect. The three women practiced in slow-motion on each other a few times, then each of them went a little harder at Tyler and Ezra.

It was past three a.m. when Ezra finally locked up his bar and they all headed out. There was no sign of the gray hatchback in the lot. She must have walked here since cabs and ride sharing apps weren't a thing out here. He suppressed a shudder that she made herself an easy target.

"You're new in town, so I'm assuming you're at the motel?" she asked.

"I am," he replied. "Can I give you a lift home?"

She shook her head. "I like to walk."

Confirmation that this was a regular thing gave him chills. "You *walk*? With guys like Jerry in the world?"

"Trust me, the world makes guys worse than Jerry."

His instincts leaped into high gear. This woman had to be Autumn. "But you walk?" he pressed. How could he confirm her identity without spooking her?

"Alone isn't all bad." Her rarely used genuine

smile flickered across her face. "Thanks for the tips." She zipped up her jacket and started off down the sidewalk.

"Please let me give you a lift," Tyler said, catching up with her.

"What if I'd rather you didn't know where I live?"

"I promise to forget the address," he said. "As soon as I drop you off."

She tipped her head up to study his face. "You're pushy."

"When the situation calls for it, yes," he admitted.

"Fine. Right now I'm at the motel too."

Resignation had never sounded sweeter. He opened the door for her and rounded the cab before she could change her mind.

"They trade me a room for housekeeping," she explained.

"Good system." They reached the motel before he'd thought of a plausible way to challenge her identity as Amber the bartender. "Which room?"

She shot him a look. "Just drop me at the office."

"Right. Caution is smart." Someday soon he hoped she could be less cautious, but he figured that would be a long process.

"It's been working for me," she said.

He parked in the space closest to the central office but she didn't rush to get out of the pickup. "Where did you learn that move?" she asked.

"During a martial arts class while I was in the Air Force."

She studied him. "Really?"

"The class or the military experience surprises you?"

"You just look too young to be a vet," she said, her gaze skittering to the sign over the motel office.

He tapped his fingertips against the steering wheel. "My original career plans shifted, but the Air Force was good to me while I served. What about you?"

"What about me?"

Now *he* needed to be cautious and tread lightly. "You look too young to be so jaded."

"My life plans changed too," she murmured.

The urge to comfort her swamped him and he barely kept himself still. The woman he'd spent every spare moment searching for was right here and he could scare her away with one wrong move. "Sounds like we've both had to hit the reset switch."

She nodded and opened the door. He followed

suit and they stood awkwardly in front of his truck. He had to pass her to get to his room and she clearly didn't want to give him any clue about where she stayed.

"Thanks for everything," she said, dashing his hopes for a more meaningful conversation. "Most people stay out of Jerry's way."

"I'm not most people."

"I noticed." That would-be smile flirted with her lips.

He gave her his room number. "If you need anything, come on by. I'll be here all week."

"There is one thing," she began.

He waited, his hand gripping the key fob tightly while his mind spun with possible requests.

"Put out the do not disturb sign," she said. "Please? One less room to clean tomorrow would be awesome."

Not the request he'd anticipated, but any chance to do her a favor was a good start. "You got it. Nice to meet you, Amber."

"You too."

He headed toward his room, refusing to glance back over his shoulder. They were the only two people out here, it would be impossible to follow her without being seen. Without crushing the seeds of trust he'd just sown.

At his room, after putting out the do not disturb sign as promised. He stripped out of his jacket, grateful he hadn't been wearing his gun tonight. Tossing his shoes into the corner, he sat down at the desk to send an email to Claudia and Swann. Once they were both up to speed, he considered his next move. Maybe now, with his name and room number attached to a helpful act and matching the note he'd left on her car, she'd come by and admit she was Autumn.

Falling into bed, he slept in fits and starts, listening for a knock at his door and dozing off to bizarre fantasies of walking down Main Street holding Autumn's hand. In those snippets of dreams, she didn't wear her wig or the makeup that blurred her features. But every time he bent his head to kiss her, Jerry jumped in and punched him.

It was a relief when sunlight slanted through the gap in the curtain and woke him up for the day. He needed some reality to erase the strange, restless night. After a shower, he walked up to the office, looking for her car, praying she hadn't run away. The car was there, but the note he'd put on it was gone. Good. On foot, he crossed the highway to the truck stop and ordered a thermos of coffee and a breakfast sandwich. The caffeine and food would keep him fueled up while he researched Jerry and his known associates.

He wasn't quite back to his room when his phone started chiming with incoming text messages from Claudia. Rather than let his sandwich go cold while he texted back, he called her once he reached his room. "What's the problem?"

"Good morning to you, too," she said. "You tangled with a known offender. Armed robbery, assault, I could go on. Why?"

"Because he was making an ass of himself and wrecking a good night at the only bar in town."

"Ty."

"How did you find out?" he wondered. He'd left the unpleasant details out of the report.

"Ty," she said again as if speaking to a grumpy toddler. "Cell phones are everywhere. You know it's my job to keep tabs on you. I use every tool at my disposal."

In her place he did the same. The sandwich turned to a sharp lump in his gut. Had he managed to expose Autumn? Some protector he'd turned into. "What did I do? Is she in danger?"

"Relax." He heard her fingers on a keyboard. "Her face is in a few shots, that's all. I don't think you blew her cover. Are you sure this is Autumn?"

"Pretty sure." As in one hundred percent positive.

"*Hm*, okay." Another few keystrokes. "The car adds up, I'll give you that."

"Gee, thanks."

"Stop being sensitive and tell me what you need to bring her in."

"Time." He wouldn't force her to do anything. She'd spent too much time with dictator types already.

"Swann set the clock for you, but you have a few more days."

He told her about Jerry wanting a private bartender for a party. "Have you pinpointed Mosley's whereabouts? I'm sure they're not fishing in the traditional sense."

"The fishing comment bothers me too. Some of the chat rooms you keep an eye on use fishing terms to cover kidnapping talk."

"I'm aware." He set the sandwich aside. Maybe it would be better cold once his appetite returned.

"You stick close to the bartender—"

"It's her."

"—and I'll see if I can figure out where Mosley might be planning to steal new girls."

"Maybe the party," Tyler suggested.

Claudia sputtered. "To push their metaphor I'd

think stealing women from a party would be more like shooting fish in a barrel than actually fishing."

Tyler didn't want to think about any of it more than necessary. The mob's actions and habits, provided in Autumn's statement, were all-too-clear in his mind. "I'm not letting her work that party."

"I would never suggest it," she assured him. "Besides it's your case. I'm just the support, remember?"

"Best around," he said. He wished he felt more like a competent bodyguard than an imposter.

"I am," she agreed. "To that end, I'm moving Hank's men a little closer."

"How? Two more strangers in town will raise suspicion." And make it more likely Autumn would disappear. "There's small town and there's wilderness and not much in between."

"I can read a map, Tyler," Claudia said, testy. "Let me do my job and you go do yours. And make sure you've got the right woman."

"Yes, ma'am."

At least Claudia was laughing when she ended the call.

Tyler was playing around with facial recognition software, trying to match Amber with Autumn when he heard the housekeeping cart rumble by. Unable to help himself, he jumped up and went to the door. He had to see her, make sure she was all right after his stunt with Jerry. Bartending and bartering for a place to stay kept her safe and fed while staying off the grid, but if he'd found her, the mob could too.

He slid back the chain and opened the door. The day was warming up nicely and the blue, cloudless sky seemed to stretch forever over the sprawling, unpopulated landscape. He leaned against the doorway until she emerged from the room two doors down, her arms full of bedding. "Good morning," he said.

She gave a little start, then a slow smile appeared. "Morning. Did you need something?"

"No, thank you. Just taking in the view," he said. He gestured with his coffee cup to the area beyond the truck stop.

"It's pretty. In a barren way."

The wistfulness in her voice tugged at his heart. He wanted to make promises that she'd get her life back and he was willing to do whatever was necessary to see that happen. Her hair was hidden under a baseball cap that matched the one on the driver up near the Blackfeet Reservation. Seeing her eyes and face without the makeup, he was absolutely certain he had found Autumn Curley.

"Do you ever moonlight as a tour guide?" he asked.

"What makes you think I know anything more than you?" she challenged.

"Wild guess, that's all," he said. "You knew the locals at the bar."

She glared at him for a long, uncomfortable moment. "I have work."

"Me too."

Neither of them budged.

"What are you doing here?" she demanded.

He couldn't let this opening slide by. "A good friend of mine is looking for her sister," he said, watching her for any reaction. She didn't flinch. "A runaway," he clarified. That caught Autumn's attention. Her nostrils flared and her eyes darted away. "We heard a rumor that she might be in this area."

"Haven't seen anyone like that here at the motel." She headed back to the room she'd been cleaning.

"I didn't even describe her," he said, following her. He stopped at the doorway, watching her work.

"You didn't have too," she snapped. "Runaways have a look. Scared rabbits." She dumped the trash into the bin in the cart and replaced the liners. "No scared rabbits in town lately."

Damn it, he'd upset her. Gone was the friendly rapport he'd worked so hard to establish last night. "Is there a place nearby where a scared rabbit could hide?"

Autumn grabbed the vacuum from the cart and slapped the cord down with a smack in the room. "Look around. No place to hide or reason to stay here." She jerked her chin toward the truck stop. "That's your best bet for anyone who might've seen her passing through. Good luck."

"Thanks. Have a good day." He turned back to his room.

She caught up with him, pausing at his door. "What will you do if you find her?"

"Reunite her with her family, if she's willing. Her dad and sister want to know she's safe," he said.

"What about her mom?" Autumn folded her arms over her chest. The loneliness in her gaze was like a slap across the face, stark and startling.

"She passed away."

"Oh." Autumn's gaze fell to the cracked sidewalk under their feet. "That sucks."

"You sound like you understand. Did you lose your mom?"

She nodded. "Why did the girl you're looking for run away?"

"Only she can answer that question."

"You'd better hope—" She caught herself and turned on her heel, walking away.

"Hope what?"

"That she's gone," she said, her tone hard as granite. "You're describing a girl that doesn't last long around here."

"Why not?"

She spun around and he was so close she nearly slammed into his chest. "It's a big nasty world, Tyler. If you don't know that already, this part of the country will show you. I need to turn over these rooms."

It was clear she wouldn't share anything else. Not right now. "Guess I'm headed to the truck stop. You know where to find me if you catch wind of her."

"Sure thing."

He bristled at the words and dismissive tone she'd used with customers at the bar last night. Telling himself that pushing harder would've backfired, he retreated. For now.

CHAPTER 6

AUTUMN DIDN'T BREATHE easy until Tyler Vidro and his truck crossed the highway. She'd learned his last name by snooping through the office register, hoping it would spark something about why he was so familiar to her.

Nothing he'd said or done had clicked. She was tempted to search his room, but if she could see his truck, he could see the motel and anyone lurking near his door. What made a man leave a military career for the thankless job of tracking down runaways?

She found it curious that he didn't offer to show her a picture of the girl he was looking for. Not that she'd been all that open to the idea. Runaways were too easy, and usually too damaged for Mosley to get a good price. Still, he'd lure them in and use them as necessary.

When she went to the office to give her report of room conditions, she asked Debbie about Tyler again.

Debbie just gave her an odd look. "You're never this interested in the guests. He was pretty curious about you too."

"W-what?" Goose bumps prickled along her skin. What if his arrival and Mosley's visit *were* connected? Had he and Jerry staged the altercation at the bar? She'd never seen Jerry give up that easily. Were they playing her? Her breakfast threatened to rise up. She had to think, remember the goal and all the precautions she had in place. "What do you mean?"

"He wanted information about the woman driving the gray hatchback. When I wouldn't give him any details, he wrote a note for me to give to you." She handed Autumn two envelopes. "He wrote two notes and tucked one under the wiper blade on your car. I took it back. Didn't want it to upset you."

Too late. A strange pressure pulsed through her system. She should escape now while she had the chance. Her tank was full and she had a decent roll of cash from her tips these last couple of weeks.

But running meant giving up a chance at Mosley and giving him room to 'fish' in this area. "He said he was looking for a runaway," she said at last.

"Oh. I got the feeling he was looking for someone."

"Me?" Autumn stared at the notes. His name and room number were written on the outside in precise lettering.

"Not looking for you, per se," Debbie said. "Whatever you're thinking, I think he's one of the good guys."

"He's a *stranger*," Autumn reminded her boss.

Debbie flicked that detail away. "We're both good at reading people. He's a veteran and honorable, whatever his reasons for asking about 'the blond who drives the gray hatchback'. You might as well read what he had to say."

"Uh-huh." Autumn had never been more grateful to hear the dryer bleating the end of the cycle. She shoved the envelopes into her back pocket and went to fold the laundry. Thankfully, Debbie didn't follow her.

Only when she was back in her room did she open the notes. Under the motel logo, he'd printed the same message on both sheets of paper.

My name is Tyler Vidro. I'm an investigator with the Guardian Agency and we're following a lead on a sensitive case in this area. We have reason to believe a young woman you might be acquainted with is in serious danger. I'd like to ask you a few questions if you have some time.

He'd provided his room number and phone number at the bottom of the notes. She dropped the papers on the bed, pacing the width of her room. Guardian Agency. That company had intervened, sending men to rescue Summer and Marnie after the safe house locations had been leaked to Mosley days before the original trial date for the men who'd kidnapped her.

That must be why she recognized Tyler, he'd been following her. She must've caught sight of his face in the background when she'd been taking out low-level gang members over this past year.

Was the line about serious danger a ploy or the truth? Only one way to find out. Taking a breath, she dialed the number he'd provided.

He answered on the second ring and she nearly jumped out of her skin. "Yeah, um. Tyler?"

"Yes."

"This is Autumn Curley." Whoops. She hadn't meant to lead with that. "Debbie just gave me the notes you left with her. For me I guess." She bit her lip to stop rambling. "She said you put one on my car, but she confiscated it."

"I see." There was a long pause. "What kind of car do you drive?"

"An old gray hatchback."

She heard his sharp inhale. "Autumn, we really need to talk," he said. "Where can we meet? I swear I'm only here to help you."

The safest place she could think of was *her* motel room, though she hated to reveal it to anyone else. Especially a man who might be on Mosley's payroll no matter how nice and sincere and legit he seemed. The prosecutor's office had been sure they were above bribes or threats too.

"Would you prefer a public location?"

"No." She gave him her room number.

"I'll be there in five minutes."

"Okay," she lied. This was so *not* okay. And not nearly enough time to brace for the shift she sensed was coming. Her goal was Mosley. Guardian Agency or not, she wouldn't be pulled from that track, not when the man was finally within reach.

FROM HIS TRUCK, Tyler sent a text message to Claudia that he was about to meet Autumn. Officially. His heart was racing by the time he parked in front of room number she'd given. Seeing the gray hatchback he breathed a sigh of relief. He'd been more than a little afraid she would run before he arrived.

He knocked on the door, and hastily removed his sunglasses, hooking them in the collar of his shirt. He hadn't felt this jittery about meeting a girl since his first date. The door swung open, but she was hidden behind it. Stepping inside, he got his first good look at her at last.

It was her. Autumn Curley without any disguise. No wig and makeup for the bartender role. No hat pulled low hiding her hair and shading her eyes as she handled the housekeeping. She'd left her hair down, a sleek waterfall of black falling past her shoulders. Dressed in a red tee with the motel logo on the front, jeans and boots, she looked young. Normal, if you ignored the wariness and suspicion blazing in her dark eyes, the sense that she would spring into an attack at any moment. Her mouth set in a straight line, no hint of any kind of smile. He was sure she had a weapon within easy reach. Probably more than one.

"Autumn." She was beautiful. The pictures in her file didn't do her justice. His heart kicked unexpectedly and he pulled himself together. "Miss

Curley," he said, starting over. He had to give her the most pertinent information before she ended this meeting. "I'm not here to cause trouble. I came to warn you that Mosely has listed you as priority number one. I'm here to escort you to safety."

She paled, backing up a step. "No."

"That was blunt. Sorry." Was she refusing his help or refusing to accept the facts?

She folded her arms and her chin lifted. "How do you know?"

"The shoplifter you dropped with tribal police on the Blackfeet reservation is Mosley's nephew."

"So he'll walk." Her eyes closed tight and when she opened them, fury blazed. "How did you figure out it was me?" she asked, eyebrows knitting into a frown. "How did you find me?"

"Combination of hard work and a bit of luck. No one saw you or has any evidence you were there," he assured her. "Honestly, everyone but your sister is willing to let you stay listed as missing. Felt that was safer for you."

Autumn sniffed. "Summer hired you?"

"Not exactly. I was part of the team called in when the Native Mob went after Summer and Marnie. And you," he added. "I've been trying to find you since the trial finished. On my own time."

"Why?" Her dark eyebrows lifted.

"Because you're a hero." He spread his arms and she braced as if she expected him to hit her. Shoving his hands into his back pockets, leaving himself open to an attack, he continued. "You exposed a serious problem the prosecutor and community is now working to address. You shouldn't be dealing with the fallout alone."

"I'm fine." She wrapped her arms around her middle. "If you found me they can too."

"They're actively searching now," he admitted. "But I don't think they're closing in yet." Unless he totally screwed up at the bar last night. That was something they could discuss later, once they were far from here.

"You did."

"Well, that's my job," he said. "You're good at covering your tracks." The compliment fell flat. Clearly, she was miserable about all of this. "Who else would be so determined to thin out the gangs?"

She rolled her shoulders. "How is Summer?"

It probably would've been better if he'd led with that, kept building the rapport rather than just dive into the deep end. "Summer is doing great. She married the bodyguard who saved her from the hitman Mosley sent out. Marnie is back at her café in Eagle Rock too."

The tension in her face eased. "Happily married too?"

"Yes, actually. To the man who rescued her," he added when she looked at him expectantly.

"Sounds like a trend." She wrinkled her nose. "I hope you didn't come after me looking for a bride." She folded her arms again. "If so, that puts you in the same league as Mosley. He sells Native girls for just that purpose."

The comparison struck him like a blow. "Mosley and I are nothing alike," he said, jaw clenched. "You won't scare me off with insults, Autumn. I'm here to protect you."

She pulled a knife from a sheath hidden at her belt and tucked it away again. "Then go. I take care of myself."

"I've noticed. And if things hadn't changed on Mosley's side, I'd let you deal with it. But his nephew will do time and he's pissed. From Mosley on down to the newest gangbanger, the whole operation is focused on finding you."

She walked over to the scuffed table and sank into one of the two chairs. "You think his return to the Crow Reservation is about me?"

He nodded.

"It's not. Mosley is here for more girls. There's a big camping event this week. Just for girls."

It confirmed what he and Claudia had suspected. "That's the fishing Jerry was talking about?"

"Yes, and I wanted to beat him senseless last night when he mentioned it. But Jerry isn't my end goal, Mosley is."

Tyler didn't care for the cold, hard emptiness in her eyes. She had murder on her mind. "And once he's gone, you'll just walk off into the sunset?"

"Something like that," she said, pressing her hands between her knees.

"Killing him puts a big target on your back. The gangs won't let you live." The local law enforcement might not look too hard, but there would be an investigation. One mistake, one random fiber left behind could land her in prison.

She shrugged, her head bowed. "Maybe I don't see the point in living."

Her voice was so low he wasn't sure he'd heard her correctly. "If you die over this, even if you kill him, he wins." He couldn't let her do it, couldn't let vengeance destroy everything she could be. "Autumn, you had a future and dreams. With the right help and time you could get all that back."

When she met his gaze the pain in her eyes slashed through him. "That was before. There's no way back, not after…"

"There *is* a way," he insisted. She bristled and he pressed on. "You survived the unthinkable." Random lines and pieces from her statement to the prosecutor skittered through his mind. "Of course it changed you. Tragedy does that. It changes everything." He wanted to touch her so badly but he didn't dare. "You survived."

"Others didn't." She shoved to her feet and crossed the room. "Others are still trapped. If I walk away now, more girls will be caught up in his net, lives ruined. I might as well join the gang myself if I do that."

He was hopelessly in over his head. Her pain was palpable. The grief over the destruction of her life and the burden of those who hadn't survived would crush her if she stayed this course. That was an unacceptable outcome and the worst of injustices in Tyler's mind. He couldn't let her carry out her plans alone.

"Let me help." She turned her back, muttering something in a language he didn't recognize. "You might as well use me, Autumn. I'm not walking away without some assurances for your sister and father."

She glared at him from over her shoulder. "Are you signing on to help me kill a man?"

If that was what she needed to hear to let him

77

stick close, he'd use it. The prosecutors across the region were doing their best to keep the gang-bangers she dropped off behind bars. Working from her statements, the Federal prosecutor had been pushing investigations to take down Mosley's operation.

None of that would be enough to convince her to change course today.

"I have resources and the full support of my agency," he said. "Consider us all at your disposal."

CHAPTER 7

FOR THE NEXT TWO DAYS, Tyler proved himself a
man of his word. If she had to have a shadow, he
was a good one. Between shifts at the motel and
her shifts at the bar they narrowed down Mosley's
possible hiding places. Tyler didn't push her to
leave the area, though she knew he wanted to. He
didn't force her to talk about what she'd been
through, instead sharing more about himself
during their drives through the national park
where girls from ten to eighteen were enjoying
their annual camping event. He and his 'resources'
were on high alert and ready to move in should a
girl be attacked or go missing.

If this was a campaign to earn her trust, it was
working. She didn't know how to feel about it.
About him. He was kind, his patience and

generosity on display at every turn. She'd laughed when he revealed his passion for high-fantasy video games and been inordinately reassured when he demonstrated excellent marksmanship skills.

She found him attractive inside and out, and that terrified her.

When she'd escaped, she vowed never to allow anyone close enough to hurt her again or worse, see the depth of her damage. Most of her scars were invisible and yet too raw to look at directly. Tyler, as a new friend and potential accomplice, tempted her to break that vow. But opening up might drive him away and that outcome would undo every inch of progress she'd made.

Following the trial, she'd expected to feel liberated. At the very least, she'd hoped to enjoy her newfound freedom, despite the ever-present threat of retaliation from the Native Mob.

Against her better judgement, she'd gone home to see her dad one last time before she disappeared. Two of Mosley's enforcers had been waiting, ready to murder her father, and destroy his property before taking her back. She'd done what was necessary to save her dad and herself. Those enforcers would never be found. Her heart had broken when she heard about the efforts made to find the missing men. Efforts that were rarely made for the girls and women Mosley plucked from their lives as easily as taking apples from a tree.

She couldn't imagine Tyler's reaction if she admitted she'd killed two men *before* she started calling in tips and delivering gang members to law enforcement offices. Did his job make him obligated to report that kind of thing?

Neither Jerry nor any of his known crew had returned to the bar since the night he'd come up short against Tyler. The gang was watching for her, she could feel it, despite the lack of solid evidence.

The Wild Bee was expecting another big crowd for the live music tonight and people were trickling in when she took over behind the bar and Tyler sat down at the end near the pass-through.

By the end of the first set they were likely over legal capacity. Her scalp itched under the wig of loose blond curls. It was a good thing her hands were too busy filling orders or she might rip it off and be done with it. Nights like this left her craving the outdoors. Space and clean air under a sky full of stars was so much better than the questionable smells of people hoping to get lucky.

She slid a glance toward her bodyguard. What

would Tyler say if she asked to sleep outside tonight? She enjoyed watching the wind ruffle his hair and the way he smiled when they were out. Better if she had the right—and the courage—to run her fingers through that thick silky hair and smooth it back into place.

Thankfully Ezra shouted out that a food order was ready, pulling her back from her dangerous, impossible thoughts.

She served the food and more drinks with her workplace smile intact while she scanned the crowd for familiar faces and signs of trouble. A fight broke out during the band's second set, but Tyler and Ezra handled it so quickly no one outside of the immediate area seemed to notice.

When the night was done, the tips counted and the bar cleaned and reset for tomorrow, she stepped out into the crisp night air with Tyler. She'd convinced him to walk over tonight and she was grateful now for the chance to stretch her legs and really breathe.

"Seemed like a good night," he said, falling into step beside her.

"Just over two hundred in tips." Ezra would pay her in cash for the hours at the end of the week. "Sure you don't want to start charging me?" she joked.

"Not sure that's legal since I'm on leave."

She really should tell him how many laws she'd broken. It felt wrong to keep dragging an honorable man into her dirty work.

"Thanks for helping with that fight," she said.

"No problem." He grinned. "Was actually kind of fun."

She recognized the sentiment. "I've been living job to job for a long time. Getting paid under the table and following rumors about the gangs."

"I know."

"That doesn't upset you?"

"If you'd tried being normal, Mosley might have found you before I did."

His easy acceptance was shocking and it unlocked something deep inside. "When they kidnapped me I vowed to resist. Every time I had to cooperate with my captors, with Mosley, felt like I was betraying myself."

"Why did he single you out?"

"You've read the statements." At his nod, she paused and looked to the sky for any kind of guidance. "I've never understood his decision. The girls thought I was lucky, but watching wasn't any better. They'd get doped up and abused and shame burned like a hot coal in my belly. I think he knew that made it worse for me."

She'd learned a wealth of hair and makeup tricks in those crowded rooms and deplorable conditions. And being sober empowered her to memorize the routes and names and details she'd given to the prosecutor.

"Probably should've moved after I nabbed the kid who was his nephew," she mused as they crossed the central intersection, utterly deserted now.

"How is it you never get caught on a security camera?" he asked. "Not closing in on your target or dropping him off."

"Family secret," she said, bumping her shoulder to his. It was the first time she'd touched a man without intent to harm since her abduction. The second time, she realized. The first had been when Tyler taught her the move that took out Jerry. "My family is famous for their tracking skills. Goes back for generations."

"But—"

"A crucial element of tracking anything is knowing the environment."

"That's not an answer," he pointed out.

"Tyler," she whispered. Across the street, there was movement in the shadows between two buildings. She'd let her attention lapse, feeling secure with Tyler nearby and now her instincts were screaming.

Three men skirted the edges of light cast by the street lamp on the corner. "Run."

"Like hell," he shot back.

"Go," she insisted. "They want me."

These three were staring at her as if they could see right through her disguise. Fear and anticipation surged through her veins, creating a strange kind of high. She liked her chances even against three grown men, but there was definitely a higher risk with Tyler involved.

They crossed the street, one of them cutting off Tyler's direct route to the motel, another coming straight at her, and the third man blocked an easy retreat. Clearly the trio didn't realize how quickly their plan to surround and crowd their targets would backfire.

She had a knife in a sheath at her ankle and another in her belt. Tyler was armed as well, though he'd left the gun behind. Too late to regret that decision now.

"Hey," the man closest to them smiled at her. She recognized him as one of the newer additions to Jerry's crew. "You always go slumming with customers?"

Tyler stretched out an arm. "Back off, buddy."

She heard the unmistakable sound of a butterfly knife opening and yanked Tyler out of the way. Not fast enough. He swore and she smelled blood. "How bad?" she asked.

"No worries," he replied.

The other two men pressed in as if the leader had chummed the water. There was nowhere to go, she and Tyler had to make a stand. "Keep the building at your back," she whispered, drawing the knife from her belt.

They would jump Tyler first, taking out what they considered the bigger threat. "Get the hell out of here before I embarrass you," she said.

The leader laughed. "Is she for real?" he asked his pals. Stepping closer, he offered his chin. "If the lady can knock me down, we'll leave."

His knife hand was loose and easy by his hip. If she got in too close, he'd take advantage and strike or slash. "Drop the knife."

"Not a chance," the leader said. "Come on, now. Everyone says you're so tough."

"Show me you'll give me a fair chance," she said, daring him. "Hold your arms out to the sides," she said.

"Don't do this," Tyler argued.

She heard a thread of pain in his voice and hoped he was thinking clearly enough to follow what she was about to do. "Come on. Or are you afraid of a girl?"

The taunting worked and the leader obliged. With her free hand, she punched him under the arm, just like Tyler had taught her a few nights ago.

The man grunted, his breath wheezing with the pain as he stumbled backward into the street. His pals leaped on Tyler and Autumn. Behind her, she heard Tyler lock up with the man between them and the motel. The third man tried to wrap her up, but she twisted, using her bodyweight as leverage.

They landed in a heap, her jaw scraping the sidewalk hard with the man on top of her. She heard a sickening crunch in her attacker's arm. He rolled away and came up on his knees, struggling to reach his gun and support his injured arm at the same time. She had the advantage, for the moment he was completely vulnerable. One plunge of her blade would kill him, but she didn't want Tyler tangled up in the murder of a low-level thug just because she couldn't control herself.

Changing her hold on the knife, she landed two quick strikes almost simultaneously, creating a shock wave in his skull that rendered him unconscious.

"You cold bitch," the leader shouted, striding

back into the fray. He shook out his arm, the butterfly knife in his other hand.

Tyler stepped in front of her and ended the fight with a blur of movement and the skittering sound of the knife sliding down the sidewalk. "Let's go." He grabbed her hand, pausing just long enough to gather up the loose weapons as they ran for the relative safety of the motel. She barely made out the shape of the man he'd fought in the shrubbery next to the corner of the store.

He headed for his motel room, but she drew him along to hers. "I keep a mobile emergency kit," she explained. Plus her room was closer to the office where any subsequent attack would be more easily overheard.

Finally, with the deadbolt and chain in place, she slumped against the door and took a deep breath. Then Tyler hit the lights and she barely smothered the scream at the sight of so much blood.

She wasn't sure her kit would be enough.

"Sɪᴛ ᴅᴏᴡɴ," Tyler barked. She looked as though she'd topple over any second and he didn't want to catch her while there was still a gangbanger's blood on his hands.

"You first," she snapped back.

The fire in her voice made him feel better, but she was still pale. The scrape along her jawline had his temper climbing. "It's not my blood." He started stripping off his jacket and shirt, tossing the ruined clothing into the bathtub. "Not all of it anyway." He was fumbling with his belt, his left hand not cooperative at all when he heard her gasp.

Damn it. She was a victim. A survivor. Either way, he was stripping in front of her without invitation. Although they won, the attack must have churned up bad memories about being in danger and defenseless. "Sorry." He backed into the bathroom and tried to close the door. "Give me a minute."

She stuck her foot in the door. "I won't faint."

"May I?" He pointed to her face. When she nodded he reached out with the hand that was working and tilted up her chin to get a better look at her jaw. "That's no fun."

"It'll be sore," she agreed.

Her dark gaze slid away from his face, down over his bared chest and over to his wounded arm. He would've sworn she'd touched him and his body reacted accordingly, his nerves hot and tingling with anticipation and a need he shouldn't feel toward a woman he meant to protect.

A woman who had seen how cruel a man could be.

"You're worse," she said, her voice husky and her eyes on his chest again.

"Am I?"

She shivered and lifted those deep, melting eyes to his face. "Well, I don't need stitches." It was oddly mesmerizing to watch her pull those shields back into place, shutting him out. Pulling a washcloth from the towel rack, she pressed it to the bleeding slice across his arm. "Keep pressure here."

"Don't do that, Autumn."

Her brow furrowed. "What?"

"Don't cut yourself off." To move on, she had to learn she could trust someone again. "You're safe with me."

She pointed at the arousal he couldn't control. Not after the fight, after the first touch of her soft skin or the way she'd looked at him. "Am I?"

"Adrenaline," he said, willing his body to cooperate.

"Huh."

He had no idea how to interpret that, so he kept his mouth shut.

After checking that the bleeding was slowing

down, she scooted around him and dragged the soiled clothing out of the tub before turning on the taps. "Clean that up and then I'll do the rest."

Steam started to rise from the hot water and he reached for his belt, fumbling with the buckle. With a sigh that brushed his skin, she took over the task, undoing his fly as well. Kneeling she dealt with his boots, tugging them off one by one. This was new territory, wishing for an erection to go away.

"Thanks," he croaked when she was done.

"You're welcome." She closed the door as she left him alone.

He managed to get out of his jeans and underwear, and made quick work of washing off the blood—his own and that of his opponent. He carefully cleansed the wound, pleased that it didn't start bleeding heavily again. Feeling better, he turned off the water and dried off, wrapping the towel around his hips.

He opened the door just a crack. "Do you mind if I'm not really decent?"

"In my experience you're all kinds of decent," she replied. "Come on out."

She'd removed the wig and makeup and changed into soft, figure-skimming pants and a plaid flannel shirt was open over a white tee. Her feet were bare and the counter was covered with a medical kit. She'd dragged a chair close to the sink. "You weren't kidding about the mobile ER."

A tentative smile bloomed across her face. "Debbie will be here any minute with clean clothes."

"All right." It was good to learn she trusted someone, even if it wasn't him.

"Attempted mugging." She dropped to one knee beside the chair. "It happens."

He let her swab the knife wound with antiseptic and hissed through his teeth at the stinging sensation that followed. "A couple of butterfly bandages should suffice, right?"

"Afraid of needles?" she queried.

"Not a fan," he admitted. "I appreciate you yanking me out of the way."

"I'm sorry you got caught in my war." She applied an ointment and the bandages, pulling the skin together on either side of the wound and then covered it with gauze. When she finished, her hand cradled his and she seemed content to linger there. "Your jacket took most of the damage," she said.

The connection fired his blood and soothed him at the same time. Until her, he'd never experienced anything like it. He tapped his chin. "Is that the worst for you?"

"It is."

"I'm glad." He couldn't drag his eyes from her face. "If you get some ice on it, it might not bruise."

"I have a cold pack." But she didn't move. "Tyler, you've done enough, so feel free to say no, but—"

"Yes."

Her lips quirked to the side. "You don't even know what I'm asking."

"Whatever it is, if I can do it, I will. For you."

She sank back on her heels, the motion taking her hand away. "When I was, um, being held by Mosley it was awful. What he did to most of the girls…"

Her voice trailed off and he waited, wishing he could erase the pain lingering in her beautiful eyes, bracketing her soft mouth.

"He didn't do as much to me. I'm not sure why. I'll never know his reasons and I don't care," she said in a rush. Pressing her hands to her face, she groaned. "I didn't have a lot of experience before I was kidnapped." Meeting his gaze again, she wrinkled her nose. "Sex was used as a weapon there. It was ugly and mean."

He fought to tamp down his fury where it wouldn't erupt and scare Autumn. He'd never wanted to kill a man the way he wanted to destroy

Mosley right now. The courageous woman who'd found a way out of the horror rose up, her eyes full of determination as her hands rested on his knees. Skin to skin. He sensed that sort of connection was as new to her as this conversation. As new as having an ally.

"I-I want a kiss. Please. Something nice," she continued. "If you won't feel used or—"

"Autumn," he cut her off gently. "Whatever you need, I'm in. Kiss me."

With heart-wrenching caution, she touched her lips to his, a whisper of warmth before she jerked back, eyes wide. Staring at him, she licked her lips.

He locked down every muscle against the instinct to draw her close. "Another?"

"Will you be mad if I say no?"

"Never." Did she realize her hands were massaging his legs? "It's your body, your choice."

She scowled at him. "It's your body and choice too."

"True." He laughed. "Sitting here in a towel makes it impossible to hide how much I want you." Dumb to draw her attention to his erection tenting the towel. "You're a beautiful woman Autumn," he continued. "I like you. I admire your tenacity and courage. You survived a hell most people can't comprehend. My choice is to do what's right for you, whenever it feels right for you."

"You're serious."

"I am."

Her eyebrows puckered again for a long moment before she leaned in and kissed him again. More sure of what she wanted this time, she gripped his shoulders as he responded, slanting her mouth over his. Sweet and needy, his pulse hammered in his ears. As her tongue swept across his, he touched her hip and she jumped again.

"That's Debbie," she said before he could muster an apology.

He heard the rapping on the door as Autumn rushed to answer and he ducked into the bathroom to regain his self-control. The women spoke for a minute, then all was quiet again.

When he stepped out of the bathroom, she practically threw his clothing at him. Apparently the kissing was over for the evening.

"Thank you," she said once he returned, fully dressed.

"It wasn't a hardship." He smiled, trying to ease the awkwardness, relieved when she smiled back. "Just so we're clear, I can be your playground," he blurted. "You're welcome to explore, discover what you like, create a healthy new sexual foundation to build on."

"That's outrageous," she murmured, her fingers tracing her lower lip. "I would never ask."

"That's why I offered." He pushed the chair back to its place at the table and looked around. She'd put the first aid supplies away while he'd pulled on clean underwear and jeans. He didn't bother with a shirt or socks since they really should get some sleep. "We need to stick together for security tonight. Which bed do you want me to take?"

"For security?" she echoed.

"Yes. Don't expect me to get pushy." She pointed him to the bed closest to the door and he checked the locks one more time before stretching out. "Get some rest, Autumn. Tomorrow we can come up with a plan."

CHAPTER 8

AUTUMN COULDN'T SLEEP, restless after that kiss, after his offer. The idea of Tyler's body becoming her personal playground was more than tempting. And he'd said her name and beautiful in the same sentence. Beauty really was in the eye of the beholder. When she looked in the mirror she still saw the ugly scars Mosley had carved on her soul. Bruises healed, but the stains of all the abuses she'd witnessed and endured remained.

How did Tyler see her so differently?

Though she tried, she couldn't shove him into the box along with most of the other men she'd met: another selfish guy out for what he could take. He'd tracked her down to save her. He was one of the good guys. It was sad how hard it was for her to accept that.

From the other bed, Tyler moaned. So much agony in that strange noise. "Tyler?" she whispered in the dark. The mattress springs squeaked in protest as he thrashed. She reached for the light on the nightstand between the beds.

He surged upright in the bed, his sky-blue eyes open, but he wasn't awake. The women she'd been locked up with often had nightmares, before they succumbed to the circumstances and drugs.

"Tyler, wake up."

He threw a wild punch and the momentum carried him back to the mattress. He curled around a pillow, his entire body rigid. She couldn't bear it. She moved to the edge of his bed and spoke his name softly. Gently she placed her hand on his shoulder, trying to soothe him. The significance coursed through her. Tyler was the first man she'd touched with affection since escaping Mosley.

His skin was warm and supple over hard muscle. How did a self-professed computer geek stay in this kind of shape? A question for another time. She spoke his name softly, mindful that he might come up swinging again at any moment. "It's just a dream, Tyler," she crooned. "Relax now. It's over. You're stuck with me."

"Autumn?"

He rolled toward her and she jumped back,

timid as a rabbit with a hawk overhead. "Yup. Just me." Goodness that gorgeous chest, dusted with dark hair, was overwhelmingly distracting.

He went very still. "What did you need?"

"Not me. You," she said. "You were having a nightmare."

"Oh." He shifted, sitting up, the sheet falling across his hips. "Sorry. Did I scare you?"

"No." She didn't mention why she was so familiar with nightmaring people. "Need to talk about it?"

"No, thanks," he replied, clearly disgruntled. "Remnant of the fight."

"Okay." She managed to ignore the surge of curiosity. "Want me to turn out the light?"

"Give me another minute if it won't keep you up."

"I can sleep through anything," she fibbed.

He arched an eyebrow but didn't challenge her claim. Was it her imagination or was he admiring her legs? She tucked herself back in, mirroring his position in the other bed.

"You weren't asleep," he said with a sexy half-smile that scrambled her brain. "Because I'm here?"

Having him in the room definitely didn't help. "I'm fine." She mentally flailed about for a diversionary topic. "Summer," she blurted. "You said my sister's happy. Are you sure?"

"Would you rather hear she's miserable?"

"Of course not." Autumn sighed. "It's just..." She'd missed so much. Although it was perfectly logical, it was tough to face the evidence of people moving on while she'd been trapped. "It's hard to reconcile in my head. What if he's not right for her and she's just got a hero complex or something?"

What if she was developing a hero complex for Tyler?

"They've got something, all right." Tyler rubbed his eyes. "Chemistry and affection all over the place. Sad, really," he joked.

She tossed a pillow at his head. He caught it, laughing. "They think they're right for each other," he said.

"I guess that's what matters." Her sister, happily married. She tried to envision it and couldn't quite succeed. Maybe if she hadn't rushed out of the courthouse the day of the trial she would've caught a glimpse of that chemistry Tyler talked about. But she'd needed to squeeze the biggest possible advantage out of every second of her head start.

"How much of the trial did you see?" Tyler asked.

"Enough." She'd watched her sister nearly break

down on the witness stand while answering questions about Autumn's abduction. "Mosley's men were determined to take me. Summer was just an unlucky witness."

He was quiet so long she thought he'd drifted back to sleep. "Autumn?"

"*Mm?*"

"Will stopping Mosely pull you out of your grief?"

She bristled. "Does this look like grief?"

"At this hour, after a nightmare, it doesn't look like much of anything."

She reached up and turned out the light. "Go back to sleep." She burrowed down under the covers and bunched up the anemic pillows under her head. Debbie should invest in a few upgrades around here. She supposed the flat pillows and thin sheets only troubled her. No one else stayed here long enough to be bothered.

In the other bed, Tyler seemed to have obediently fallen asleep. The fact did nothing to help her mood. Sleeping after a nightmare was impossible for her, even if she hadn't been the one caught in the bad dream. Rolling to her back, she wished she was outside, staring up at a diamond-studded velvet sky rather than the stained ceiling. For as long as she could remember, she preferred sleeping outside. She felt small, but safe under that vast expanse. Her time as a prisoner left her with claustrophobic tendencies in addition to the other issues she was trying to shed. Time outside was essential to her healing, to creating that new foundation Tyler mentioned.

"You'll be fine, too."

Tyler's voice, faint and dreamy, startled her. "Will I?"

"*Mm-hm.*"

She wasn't so sure. Unless she took Mosley out, she would always be looking over her shoulder for the next person he sent to hunt her down. The king of the gangs threw around money and influence, harassing people until they broke down. He found their weaknesses with unerring precision and stomped them to bloody pulp until resistance wasn't even a logical consideration.

"What happened to the person in the prosecutor's office who leaked the witness locations?"

"Team effort," Tyler said, his tone indicating he was wide awake now. "We figured it out and charges were filed."

She waited for more, but the lack of an ending to the story made the result clear. "And the Native Mob handled it."

"Yes," he confirmed. The bed squeaked as Tyler

changed positions. "I'm sorry we haven't locked up Mosley for you."

"He'll continue to get a free pass because most people can't stand up to him or his tactics," she muttered.

"But you can?"

Yes. She'd never been so close to a clean take-down. "So far I've thrown a few wrenches into the operation, but it doesn't make much impact. The money from trafficking is too good for him to quit entirely."

"You intend to kill him?"

Why deny it? "Yes." She wouldn't rest easy until the head of the snake was severed. "Does that change your intention?"

"No." The mattress squeaked and suddenly the light came on, shining in her face.

She squinted against the glare. "A little warning?"

"Sorry." Lying on his side, he propped his head on his fist. "I intend to protect you from Mosley. During my service I was proud of the work I did personally and as a team. We took a lot of crap because we weren't boots on the ground. They thought we had it easy."

She was glad for the light now. The furrow between his brows and the distant look in his eyes gave her a better understanding of the significance here. She'd always been good at reading body language, but being a captive had honed those skills even more. Something haunted him.

"Remote or not," he continued, "there is nothing easy about watching the wrong people get caught up in an airstrike. Innocent lives were cut short because of my work."

"So you're boots on the ground today out of guilt?" she wondered.

"No. I'm here because you survived. I'm here because you need someone watching your back while you try to save others."

She never expected anyone to understand the only healing path she could see. Freedom was cheap if others were still trapped. "I survived," she agreed.

"I'm here because your life is worth more than this quest for vengeance."

"Bull. You can't say things like that." She shot up out of the bed. "All my dreams were crushed inside Mosley's hell. And I *did* have it easy." She paced the narrow space between the beds. "The justice system let me down. Two men went to prison, but Mosley keeps stealing women. I can't go back to the frivolous goals I had before."

"What did you want before?"

"Stupid stuff. A career with the parks, a husband, a-and kids." She wrapped her arms tightly around her middle. "Meaningless stuff."

"That has meaning. You can still have it all."

"No." She shook her head. "Time isn't the issue. The prosecutor took me to the best doctors. Had me tested for substance abuse and dependency, ran bloodwork for STDs." She pushed at her hair. "The works. As far as STDs I was clean. For whatever reason, the drugs didn't have as much of an effect on me. Some genetic glitch or bonus—depending on your perspective—saved me from the worst of it. I used that small advantage, intervening for the others as much as possible."

`All the ugliness she kept bottled up spilled out. "One day I went too far and took a hard beating from the guards that nearly killed me." Now an elbow and her hip ached when it rained. "Mosley was furious. He'd been negotiating to sell me and I was damaged."

"How damaged?"

"Enough. The bones healed, but... I have scar tissue inside," she rested a hand on her belly. "It will prevent a healthy pregnancy." She sank down on the edge of the bed, refusing to look at him. She didn't want to see pity in his beautiful eyes. "They offered to remove everything, but I couldn't."

"Of course you couldn't," he said immediately. "One expert—"

"A team," she corrected.

"One *team* of experts doesn't know everything."

She wanted to throw herself into his arms for those words alone. "If you'd been there, you would've been the only person to support my decision. They assumed I didn't understand the ramifications."

"A body is more than technical."

They agreed on that. "It felt like if I gave up those parts, Mosley would win one more round."

"He hasn't won anything," Tyler said, his tone full of venom. "Not then and not now." He was out of the bed and pacing as she had done. "I assumed you were full of revenge and rightly so. But this makes me want to drag him across a gravel road for a few miles before you can have him."

"That'd be great entertainment." She smiled, almost laughed. "I watched them make the first raid after the trial. The satisfaction didn't last," she admitted.

"They saved ten women," he said.

"I know." That fleeting satisfaction dogged her more and more. Would she ever find fulfillment, a way to make a lasting difference? "It won't be enough for me until Mosley's done and the whole mess dismantled." That was step one.

"All right." Tyler fastened his jeans and pulled on his clean jacket without a shirt. "It's time to make that happen."

"Where are you going?"

He stomped into his boots. "To my room. I work when I can't sleep. We need to figure out if and when he'll attack that girl's camp."

"When," she said. There were no ifs when Mosley talked of fishing. "Hang on. I'll come with you."

He paused, studying her in silence as she dressed.

"I don't want to be alone." She joined him at the door and on a silly whim, kissed him again. Her head was light, her heart fluttering against her ribs, when she eased back.

"You don't ever need to be alone again," he said softly, his hand sifting through her hair. "It will always be your choice."

She desperately wanted to be strong enough to choose him.

CHAPTER 9

"WHAT ARE YOU DOING?" Tyler asked, turning from his laptop to watch her.

"The motel room is too small," she lied, focusing on the task of lacing up her hiking boots. "Need to breathe."

She tried to label her reaction as a simple adjustment to having him here in her space. They'd moved in Tyler's gear less than twenty-four hours ago, for mutual safety and easier cooperation to plan Mosley's takedown.

But there was nothing simple about this frantic need to stay close to Tyler. She enjoyed his company so much it frightened her. "I need a night under the stars."

"Do you?"

"Yes." She stood and faced him. Her hair was

braided back from her face and all her disguises were gone. *This* was the real her. Or the closest she'd found post-Mosley.

He studied her with that cool sky-blue gaze while she struggled not to fidget or speak, waiting for his rejection.

"You expecting to fight off a bear for the right to sleep outside?"

She'd thought Tyler was too distracted with his work to notice the weapons she'd strapped on under her gear. "It's possible. Safety first." She grabbed her backpack.

"Especially if the bear is working for the Native Mob, right?" He got up from the table and blocked the door, his arms folded over his chest.

How could she make him understand she needed to deal with her demons her way? "Most bears are good bears," she said. "I'm just prepared."

"Autumn, you're prepared for a war."

He had no idea. Ezra had called to ask her to come in after overhearing Cici's plans for a big girls' night while Jerry was away on his fishing trip. Mosley would strike tonight or tomorrow. "Move, Tyler. I'll be back in the morning."

He didn't oblige. "Tell me what you've heard and we'll call the authorities to handle it. It's time to let someone else take over this fight."

"They won't." Her voice cracked. She mimicked his pose, crossing her arms. "They won't act on a vague tip in time to make a difference. I can and I will."

"You've done this alone for long enough, Autumn. What happened to team effort?"

"I can't." A team put more people at risk. "I expected you to understand."

"I do." He lifted his hands and then tucked them quickly into his pockets before he touched her. "I thought I did. Talk to me."

Why did she suddenly resent that thoughtfulness? Oh, yeah. Because he touched her with affection and warmth. The desire she felt in his hands and lips wasn't about greedy possession, it was about honoring *her* wishes, giving her the space and confidence Mosley had stolen. They hadn't done more than kiss, but she'd never known kissing could feel so incredible all over.

"I have to do this, Tyler. Let me go and I'll talk to you when I get back." It would hurt to watch a girl get kidnapped, even for a few hours, but that would lead her straight to Mosley and the end of this obscene organization.

Tyler still didn't budge. Exasperated, she erupted. "What good is a call or a team? Talking hasn't fixed anything. The official raids haven't put a dent in Mosley's operation. 'Scarcity is profit', he used to say." She shuddered at the memory.

"It's going down tonight? You're sure."

She saw the fiery temper in his eyes. "Yes." She explained Ezra's call first, adding what she'd learned inside. "Mosley's men bragged about snatching girls from this kind of event and leaving just enough of a trail to give searchers false hope. I can follow the real trail."

Tyler scowled. "Why don't these groups take better preventive measures?"

"They do. He doesn't strike the same event often. Personally, I think he only fishes at these big events when he has a special order."

Tyler paled. Finally, she was getting through. "What if you're the special order this time, Autumn?"

An unsettling thought, but one she had considered. "Then I'm right where I want to be, facing off with Mosley."

"He wants you dead."

"For good reason," she agreed. "But he doesn't have anyone on the payroll who can see me coming."

Clearly Tyler wasn't convinced. It was a refreshing change to study someone for the joy of it, without fear of an incorrect interpretation leading to abuse. "The people who place orders are sick and ugly and become the harsh reality for too many girls," she said. "Let me get out there and stop this. If he can't fulfill the order, maybe he'll be pissed off enough to come out from under his rock and face me personally. Then we can haul his sorry ass to the authorities."

"And that will be enough?"

She hoped so. "Yes. With Mosley out, the operation will crumble."

Or be much easier for her to dismantle. Her life had become a cheap commodity since taking up vengeance against the Native Mob. She was willing to put her life on the line, as long as Mosley died first.

"Fine," Tyler said, relenting. "But I'm coming along."

No." she shook her head. "You'll slow me down."

He snorted. "For the next two minutes. Maybe."

While she watched, impatient, he geared up with remarkable speed, surprising her when he added a knife and a gun before gesturing to the door. "Waiting on you now."

Impressed, she turned and walked out, hiding her smile.

İf Ṫyler hadn't known Autumn was beside him, he never would've spotted her. She blended into their hiding place that well. Somehow it seemed as though her breaths were timed with the soft breeze that sighed through the trees. Down in the valley there had to be a hundred tents, each of them full of girls, chaperones, and camp leaders. How did Mosley expect to succeed?

"He won't do the dirty work himself," Autumn murmured. "And whoever he sends to blur the trail won't be as good as me."

"Us," he reminded her.

"Us." Her reluctant agreement would've amused him under different circumstances.

She'd insisted they focus on the end of camp closest to the wilderness. It made sense, giving the kidnappers an easier escape route. Still, it felt like a lot of ground to keep an eye on.

"They're typical predators," she murmured in a flat tone that got swallowed up by natural night sounds. "Cull the weak. Easier to control and easier for the buyer to mold."

The things she said, so casually, chilled his blood. If he got close enough to put hands on anyone in this gang, he would make every blow count.

"There." She handed him the binoculars. "Tree line, two o'clock."

He didn't see anything right away, but with Autumn practically vibrating with energy he kept scanning the area. Spotting movement that didn't fit with the breeze, he watched, horrified, as three men neared rows of tents. They rippled through the shadows, steering clear of the few lights, and stopped between two tents that were already dark.

Tyler listened, anticipating an alarm. But this wasn't a military installation. No one was standing watch.

Autumn tapped his arm. "Call it in. I'll get close enough to follow."

Like her, he hated that these evil men would touch an innocent child, even for the short time needed to make the rescue. At least he'd convinced her to amend her original plan of tracking the kidnappers back to Mosley. Tonight they'd leave the kidnappers trussed up in the woods for law enforcement and return the potential victim to the camp.

As Autumn faded into the night, Tyler called the county sheriff's office. When the deputy on duty answered, Tyler identified himself as a chaperone at the camp and reported three strange men loitering nearby. He ended the call before he was forced to tell more lies in the interest of justice. He stashed the phone and binoculars into the small backpack and left it at the observation point to pick up on their way out. Assuming they both got out of this in one piece.

He found her waiting, crouched low, her gaze on the shadows where the men were still lingering. "What are they waiting for?" he asked. She didn't reply.

Two men went inside the tent while one stood watch. Tyler listened for a scream, hoping one of the girls would be able to fight back enough to raise a ruckus and bring in help.

The man standing watch accepted something shoved at him from inside. Something that looked remarkably like a sleeping bag zipped around a body. He slung it over his shoulder and set off for the trees. Tyler's stomach knotted. If the bundle *was* a girl, it was distressingly still.

The other two men emerged, hurrying away from the camp. One of them with a bundle on his shoulder similar to the first.

Autumn cursed and pulled the knife from the sheath at her belt. Too close to the camp for his gun, Tyler drew his knife and they set off after the kidnappers. She must've been as antsy as he was because she intercepted the men much sooner than planned. Without a word to him, she rushed forward and tackled the last man in the line. She used the bundle to block her approach and took him down so that his body would cushion the girl's fall.

Tyler trusted her to hold the advantage as he ran past her and leaped on the man who wasn't carrying anything. From the corner of his eye, he caught a glimpse of the first man running off with the prize.

Damn it.

He didn't have much time to dwell on it when his opponent bucked him aside, rolling to his feet. Moonlight bounced off a wide blade and Tyler braced for a battle.

In the dark, the sounds of the struggle between Autumn and the other man were hard to ignore. He couldn't waste time here. Charging forward, he slid feet-first into the other man. The kidnapper lost his grip on the knife and Tyler took control of his unarmed opponent quickly. Pinning him down with a knee, he cuffed him with plastic zip ties Autumn had provided.

The woman knew her stuff.

He looked around for the next threat and found

himself on the wrong end of a shotgun. Was this the third man on the crew or someone they hadn't counted on? Didn't matter. The sheriff could sort it out. Tyler threw his knife, praying it either landed true or impeded the man's aim.

An agonized grunt and a wild gunshot that chewed through the trees overhead confirmed he'd found the mark despite the deep shadows. The bigger worry was who would react and how? Would the gunshot bring backup for the crew or innocent people from the camp?

Once again, Autumn's opponent was unconscious. "You have to show me how you do that," he said.

She secured him and scrambled toward the sleeping bag he'd dropped. "Get the idiot who fired and come back for her. I'll track the other girl."

"On it," he said, rushing toward the gunman. The man had dragged himself toward a fallen log but he wasn't nearly as good at camouflage as Autumn. Tyler had control of the gun and the man restrained in less than a minute. That done, he retrieved his knife from the man's thigh.

"You won't get away with this," the man shouted as Tyler left him behind.

He returned to where he'd left Autumn, only to find the sleeping bag unzipped, and a lumpy sack of fabric where he'd thought a young girl had been. What the hell?

He swore. This had been a trap for Autumn and Tyler had let it happen. He stood, turning in a circle. She was the tracker, the expert out here. How would he find her?

A sharp whistle cut through his thoughts and the trees seemed to come alive, trunks splitting as men showed themselves, surrounding him. An eerie quiet fell, as if everyone was holding their breath waiting for the next signal. It took every ounce of willpower not to shout her name. Did they already have her?

He was in over his head. One gun, two knives, and no clear escape route. Where was Autumn? Helpless, he could only pray the sheriff's department had taken his call seriously.

He heard a gasp and a thud as something landed hard in the dirt. Moving only his eyes, he tried to see what had fallen. An owl screeched and then something whizzed through the air, coming way too close to his cheek. Behind him a scream of pain was followed by a flurry of commotion.

"Run!"

Autumn's command rang through the night. He raced toward their original route into the camp, trusting her completely. He tripped over a body, regained his feet, and kept going. Passing a big tree, she stepped out with a compound bow and shot an arrow toward the men behind him.

"Keep going," she said a moment later, catching up with him.

He grabbed the pack he'd left earlier and stayed the course. From the sounds behind them, they would be caught within minutes, before they could get to his truck. How could he protect her from Mosley now?

"Pay attention!" Urgent and low, he would've run off without her if she hadn't grabbed his sleeve.

As it was, he nearly fell into her when she pulled him down into the deep shadows of an uprooted tree. She pressed her finger to her lips in the universal sign for silence, but he didn't have any intention of talking. Not until they were well out of danger.

He didn't trust his thoughts to come out in the right order, didn't trust her to hear him out when he made a mess of all the things he wanted to say. Had she killed the man he tripped over, or the man she'd put an arrow into? He didn't really care. His greater concern was how much more she could bear. He'd meant it earlier when he said it was time for her to leave the fight to others.

Where in the hell was the sheriff's department?

After the first stampede of booted feet passed by she guided him further from their original track. It would've been a pleasant night hike if not for the threat of a gang willing to kill him to take her.

When the trees parted, revealing a short rocky waterfall, she stopped. Drawing him closer to the water's edge to sit with her, the cool mist felt good on his face.

"Breathe," she said. "They won't find us here."

"But they'll find your car."

"So what?" She pushed her hand into her hair, then started to unravel her braids that kept it out of her face. "Nothing valuable there. I think it's clear they've known where I was for a while now."

"I suppose." His heart rate slowly came closer to normal. "What now?"

"How about a decent night's sleep under the stars?" she suggested.

Personally, he'd rather have a tent, but it was a clear night. "Why do you think the sheriff's department didn't show?"

"They probably did. We made enough noise that they'll do a headcount at the very least."

That seemed woefully inadequate. What would it take to really stop Mosley?

"You're thinking too hard." She crawled into his lap, her thighs bracketing his.

He was instantly hard, adrenaline only intensifying everything he felt for her. He wanted to hold her close, feel her heart beating against his, taste the forest and moonlight on her skin.

His palms tingled, eager to touch, but he managed to hold back, keeping his promise to let her set the pace.

She lifted his hands and brought them to her lips before laying his palms over her breasts. Her soft moan at the contact sent a wildfire raging through him. Leaning forward, she kissed him.

Nothing hesitant this time as her lips played over his and her tongue stroked boldly into his mouth. She tasted sweet and wild. He let her guide his hands where she needed his touch, let her hands roam over him as well, cautious of the weapons they carried.

He didn't have a condom with him, but maybe that was for the best, he couldn't get too carried away.

She opened his fly and her hand closed around his shaft, stroking him base to tip and back again. He swallowed an aching plea for more, resisted the urge to reverse their positions. He'd made her a promise. Couldn't go back on his word.

"Can I?" she asked.

He looked up into her face, saw her nibbling her lip. Indecisive had never looked so sexy. He eased a hand up along her neck. When she didn't flinch, he gently drew her in for a kiss. "Can you what?"

He would've sworn she was blushing, though it was impossible to tell in the near dark.

"Kiss you." She gently squeezed his erection. "Here."

He *would not* go back on his word, though this would be a test. "Yes," he managed. He had to find the control to hold himself in check. She wriggled down his body, her breath teasing his sensitized flesh. He rooted his hips to the ground, refusing to scare her off by bucking into her mouth.

Her first touch was a light kiss that nearly blew him apart. Then her tongue lapped at him. The combination of velvet heat and shyness was almost too much to bear. He dug his fingers into the soft earth as her mouth closed over him, taking him deep as she glided up and down his shaft. He stifled a groan.

Her lips danced up and down his length, feathering kisses all over before she sucked him deep once more. He was on the verge and didn't want to ruin what was supposed to be a fun exploration. "Autumn. Stop. Please."

She looked up at him, her hair rippling over one shoulder, tickling his stomach and hip. "I'm doing it wrong?"

"No." He toyed with her hair.

"Oh." A sly smile curved her luscious mouth. "I'd like to keep going. To see what happens. How it feels when..." Her voice trailed off as she bent her head to lick him again.

She'd kill him. "I've had enough close calls for one night." He shifted, drawing her body along his and distracting her with kisses that were much safer for both of them.

She wouldn't be deterred. "You said—"

"A lot of stupid things."

Her fingers slipped under his shirt and skimmed along his ribs over his hip until she was pressed even closer. "I want to know how you feel. Inside me."

He rested his forehead on hers. "I don't have a condom."

"I can't get pregnant, remember?"

If anything would cool him down, that was it. They'd hurt her, irrevocably. Brutally. She was only asking him to hold up the bargain they'd made and let her reclaim her body and discover what healthy, consensual sex should be.

"I swear I'm clean." She sat up. "I wouldn't lie about that."

"*Shh*. I trust you," he assured her. When she relaxed, he kissed her again. "Out here? You're sure about this?"

"Yes."

He supposed out here under a night sky full of stars was exactly where Autumn should be when she chose to reclaim her body and reset her sexual history.

"And you're sure we won't be found by anyone?"

She smiled again. "Not here."

"Then consider the playground open."

Her laughter was the sexiest sound he'd ever heard. She leaned into him and between hot kisses and needy touches they shed their clothing, using some pieces as a blanket. He let her set the pace at every turn, until at last she straddled him again. He was thrilled when she leaned forward so he could kiss and nuzzle her breasts. Positioned over him, she slowly sank down, taking him inch by inch into her silky, wet heat. She lifted his hands to her breasts again and he watched and listened for every clue about how to please her.

He'd never given so much control to another person and though he wanted to take over, to show her more, he managed to keep his word. For her.

Her hips pumped in quick jerky motions, then slower, deeper as her body clenched tightly around him. She tested different angles and pace. Tested his resolve. He caught her hand and moved it between them, guiding her fingertips to that tight bud of nerves at the apex of her sex. She gasped and hesitated. Resistant to him or what she was feeling?

When he'd agreed to let her lead he hadn't known how much he would crave touching her. She was beautiful, though she struggled against that truth too. It was impossible to see her expression in the darkness, her face hiding in deeper shadows cast by her hair as she leaned down to kiss him. "Will you take over and touch me like I'm a normal woman?"

"You're sure?" His heart ached for what she'd lost.

At her nod, he sat up, bringing her fully onto him, relishing in her startled gasp. He felt her smile as he kissed her, pouring himself into that mutual contact. Feeling her relax, he traced her spine, down to her hips and back up to her nape. Over and over until she was swaying into the motion. This time when he touched her clitoris, she bucked hard, her fingers digging into his shoulders.

He let her push him back to the ground, let her grind against him while he caressed her all over. She was so close, her breath short and hips pumping as she chased a climax. He was at the edge himself. Thrusting upward when she arched back, they found that peak together, her body bathed in moonlight, her hands locked with his for balance.

The pleasure with her eclipsed everything he'd known before and left him longing for a woman, an intimacy, he wasn't sure he could claim.

AUTUMN WANTED to sing or dance or shout with joy. Instead, with Tyler still buried deep inside, she stretched her arms to the sky and gave thanks. This beautiful moment would now be her official first experience.

He was perfect. She felt utterly, beautifully shattered. All the small pieces of herself were suspended, hanging in the air like dust motes in a sunbeam. As each separate bit met another, came together, she felt remade. New, whole. Right.

Her thighs quivered when she finally moved to stretch out beside Tyler. Heat from his body warmed her all over, filling her with a languid pleasure that was almost as wonderful as the orgasm.

She didn't deserve the good luck of being found by Tyler, but she wouldn't push him away. Should she say thank you? That sounded wrong in her head, so she kept the words to herself and snuggled closer.

For the better part of two years sex had been nothing more than a demonstration of violent control. Tyler had just shown her it was possible to create something different. Something healthy and wonderful. A man's arousal didn't have to mean pain or humiliation. She hadn't been sure she could even reach a climax any more, afraid those bleak months of captivity had ruined her forever.

Until Tyler had agreed to be her safe playground.

Thank you. She said the words in her head as he curled his body around hers. Shelter and strength. Warmth and comfort. His presence even made a night under the stars better.

GLORIOUS WAS the word that came to mind when Tyler could think again. He wrapped himself around Autumn and held her as tightly as he dared. Soon they would have to hike out of here, she couldn't mean to stay out in the open all night, without shelter.

"We should probably move," she said.

He had no idea how much time had passed since the fight in the woods or the incomparable sex. "Probably." Should he ask how she was doing or point out how content she seemed to be in his embrace? He eased close enough to brush his lips to the soft skin behind her ear.

She flinched and scooted away.

Too far. He supposed the line between just enough and too much would be razor thin for a long time.

She rolled over and touched her nose to his. "Sorry."

"Don't apologize to me," he said. "I'm just the playground."

Her lips brushed across his. "Don't say *just*. You've given me an amazing gift."

It shocked him how much he wanted her to keep him forever. If an affectionate gesture was crossing the line, making that declaration would obliterate it.

"Thanks for treating me like a normal person."

"You are normal," he said. "Everyone has been through something."

Propping her head on one hand she traced designs on his torso. It tickled and turned him on in equal measure. "My demons are big and mean."

"You're stronger, you'll overcome." She had too much grit and courage to give up or give in.

"I hope you're right." The wind gusted and she shivered. "Let's get dressed and settle in."

"You really want to sleep out here?" he asked. "Without a tent?"

"Please? It's a mild night." She sat up and started sorting the clothing, shimmying into her panties. "We aren't any interest to the animals out here."

He wasn't so sure, but he couldn't muster up an argument, not while satisfaction was heavy in his system.

Dressed again and tucked up together out of easy view, Tyler watched the stars winking in the night sky between the towering trees. Sleep eluded him. They'd come for her, just as he feared. Mosley had elevated his strategy to a new level, using what she'd learned inside the operation against her.

They weren't dealing with a clever criminal with an eye for profit. When it came to Autumn, it seemed the bastard wanted revenge more than money. That made him more dangerous than ever.

She would never walk away from the fight. Even if he could convince her, it was clear to him now that she'd never be safe while Mosley was free. Tyler wouldn't—couldn't—allow her to throw her life away in the process of taking out the bad guy.

"You can't keep taking these chances," he whispered.

"I can't let him keep stealing my sisters."

No, she couldn't. "I'm not asking you to do that. I'm saying we need a better plan."

CHAPTER 10

THE NEXT MORNING, as they hiked back to where they'd left her car, Autumn felt the fight from the night before in every fiber of her body. Tyler was right about the camp being a trap, but Mosley had stolen girls that way in the past. She wasn't a grand strategist, able to plot effective counter attacks. At the moment she only wanted to take Mosley out.

Somehow, she'd thought the universe would cooperate more with her determination to rid the world of a bastard like Mosley. She had a better idea now of where he was holed up on the reservation. They just needed confirmation. How could she get Tyler to help with that search?

When they reached her car, her mind switched to finding the quickest way to coffee and a hearty breakfast. They'd already killed the emergency granola bars she'd packed while they hiked the long way around to avoid gang members left on patrol.

"What the hell?" Tyler pulled a paper from under the windshield wiper.

"A ticket?" she asked, knowing it wasn't when his eyes snapped up and scanned the horizon as he turned in a full circle. "What?"

He crumpled the paper and opened the door. "Wait over there." He pointed to the trees and then dropped to his belly, looking under the car.

"What is it?" She crouched next to him. "Native Mob isn't so into car bombs."

"No?" He glared at her hard enough that she backed up. "And they never change tactics, right?" He checked the undercarriage and then stood up, dusting off his hands.

"Can I see what spooked you? Please?"

"In the car. If someone's watching I'm done putting on a show."

"All right." She figured they were safe. If Mosley's crew was close they'd attack, especially after the embarrassment of not catching her last night.

She held her breath as she turned the key, but the engine started up without trouble. Tyler was still glaring at everything in sight. "The note?" She held out her hand.

He gave it to her.

The note was a call for a truce. "He wants to meet at the diner tomorrow."

"I can read," Tyler grumbled. "Obviously he's known your location for a while."

"That was clear when they jumped us the other night." It had mystified her that another crew hadn't come at her in the days since. Of course, Tyler's constant presence made it harder to over-power her or corner her.

"Right."

"You know I have to go," she said.

"Not alone." His hands were curled into fists, balanced on his knees. He was rattled.

She sympathized. While the note wasn't an outright threat, she knew Mosley had no good intentions toward her. She'd cost him too much money and pride.

If the roles were reversed, she'd be upset about Tyler on a solo meeting with a dangerous man. Was that an unexpected by-product of having great sex?

"We'll make a plan, but we can't ignore this," she said. "If he shows up—"

"He can be arrested." Tyler's blue gaze held hers. "Do you really think he'll crawl out from under his rock and make himself available to the authorities?"

Not a chance. She put the car in gear and left the state park behind. "We'll think of something."

He snorted and then stayed quiet for the rest of the drive to the motel. She parked and cut the engine, but neither of them moved to go into her room.

"Is all this extra angst about last night?" She suddenly felt more exposed than when she'd actually been bare in front of him. "My sister told me sex changed things between people. Is that what's happened here?"

"No." He swore under his breath. "Yes." There was a flicker of amusement in his eyes when he faced her. "I've never met anyone as brave or candid as you. In actions or words."

"Meaning I'm a problem."

"Don't put words in my mouth, Autumn." He scrubbed at his face. "Your candor is a good thing. If you haven't always been that way, then maybe it's best to call it a good outcome after a lot of bad things."

It was an intelligent perspective, one she'd appreciate more if she didn't think he'd use her agreement against her.

"The truth is I came out here to protect you from Mosley. Maybe it started as some kind of hero complex or a way to counter my past. That's not what it is now. To be candid, you matter to me. I care about you and I don't want to see Mosley use your natural strengths against you."

She didn't know what to say. She would treasure those words when this was over and she had time. Right now, if she looked too closely, she'd get overwhelmed and too distracted to plan anything. When it came to Mosley, she needed a clear head and every ounce of steel she could find in her spine.

"Let's go in and clean up. We can talk this out over breakfast," she said. "Not the diner," she added, anticipating his next question. "We'll raid the kitchen down at the bar."

She wasn't ready to share a shower, though Tyler's body tempted her. He let her have the bathroom first while he filed a few reports.

"Two deputies did go out to the camp," he said in passing as he stripped off his boots and shirt. "They took statements from people who heard the fight in the woods, but everyone was accounted for so they held off the search until this morning."

Her questions had to wait until he was done in

the shower. "No one was hurt or missing?" she asked.

"That's right." He laced up his shoes and grabbed his keys. "The tent was an extra in the row."

What did that mean? She pondered it as they drove down to the bar. She unlocked the delivery door and locked it behind them once they were inside. "He staged that whole scene? How?" she mused.

"I'm guessing the same way he exposed three secure witness locations. Leverage and money."

"I feel like an idiot."

"You shouldn't. You were focused on a worthy cause, that's all."

She wasn't so sure. Gathering eggs and bacon from the cooler, she directed Tyler toward the bread and potatoes. "Skillet hash work for you?"

"Absolutely."

"Good." She lifted a deep skillet from the rack on the wall. "All this time I've been playing right into his hands."

"A game of cat and mouse with a wounded tiger," Tyler agreed. "The diner is a trap."

"But it's so public, I don't see how that works in his favor." She started the bacon and then they scrubbed and peeled a few potatoes. They continued to work side by side like a well-oiled machine until the hash was ready.

They ate in the kitchen where they wouldn't be spotted by anyone passing by. Not that too many people came to this end of town so early in the morning.

"If I don't go to the meeting, he'll escalate," she began, thinking out loud.

"And the next step up from attempted murder is?"

Murder. Death. End of her story.

A week ago she might've been ready to go out in a blaze of glory, as long as she took Mosley with her. Tyler changed that more than she was ready to admit over a morning-after breakfast.

"Then what do you think I should do? Skipping the meeting might keep me safe, but someone will pay. The man literally beats out his frustrations on people. He chooses people who won't or can't fight back." She'd seen it time and again when Mosley wasn't happy with the bottom line.

"I don't want that either. We'll think of something."

She looked down to see him holding her hands, stroking away the tension. With a gentle tug, she pulled away. Leaning on him was a foolish move. What would she do when they parted ways?

And they had to part ways. Life—or death—would soon take them in different directions. She was too damaged to be part of his world and he was too honorable to keep hunting criminals with her.

"I'll meet him at the diner," she stated, ignoring the dismay in his gaze. "We know it's a trap of some sort. How do we turn it around in our favor?"

Tyler pushed a hand through his hair and pulled out his phone, setting it between them on the stainless steel work table. "If I had a vote in this, I'd call in backup I could trust. A team Mosley doesn't know."

"All right." That was common sense. "What would you have the backup do?"

"Watch the front and back doors."

"Cutting off his escape routes."

Tyler nodded. "Would be nice to have someone inside the diner too."

"You don't plan to be there?" That surprised her, unnerved her more than a little.

"Oh, I'll be there. I just meant someone else that he doesn't recognize as your ally." He drummed his fingers on the counter. "Better for everyone if you wore a wire."

She saw it too clearly in her mind, Tyler and Mosley facing each other across one of the scarred table tops in the diner. That would not end well for either man, but Tyler was naturally fair. Mosley wasn't. The king of the mob would chew him up and spit him out in pieces and that would destroy her.

Tyler couldn't be at the meeting. She had to find another way.

"You really think he'll confess anything with you close enough to overhear?" She shook her head. "Not a chance."

"We'll see."

She couldn't decide if she was impressed or intimidated by the casual confidence. "After last night, I'd be a fool to turn down any help," she said. What was he thinking? "I can't imagine he'll actually show up, live and in person. He has lieutenants and lackeys for that. Let's forget the wire." Then no one would hear her promising to kill him in slow, excruciating ways.

He gave her a long, assessing look as she gathered up the dishes. "Can't leave a mess for Ezra," she said.

She had a less than a day to figure out how to keep Tyler away from that meeting. How could she hide her true intentions from a man who saw right through her? It wasn't at all fair since she had such a hard time understanding herself these days.

CHAPTER 11

IT MUST HAVE BEEN the silence that woke Tyler early the day of the meeting. Silence and the sheets that were cool to the touch where he'd expected to find Autumn's warm and supple body. After making love in a bed this time, he'd dozed off, to the soothing sound of her sated breathing, his body tangled with hers.

That incredible sense of peace was gone now.

"Autumn?" he called softly. He listened, hopeful for any sound.

Nothing.

Sitting up, Tyler looked around the dark room. He was alone. Knew it without turning on a light. Frustration and worry coiled tight in his gut. With an oath, he threw back the covers and stalked to the bathroom. That door was open, no sign of her.

She'd left.

Damn it.

Where was the trust? Why had he thought she'd stick to the plan they'd worked out with Claudia and Hank's men?

He was a sappy idiot, blinded by his feelings for her. Feelings that went deeper than simple infatuation or curiosity, or even an objective pursuit of answers about her case. He had fallen in love with her and he didn't care if she didn't feel the same way. He believed that he'd earned her trust at the very least. He thought he could trust *her*. It was ridiculous to be this wrong about a person.

Of course, she'd gone out on her own. *Of course*, she'd followed her gut rather than their plan. Not once had she volunteered to work with him. He'd had to force the issue at every turn.

Well, he wasn't giving her a choice. She couldn't meet Mosley alone and expect to survive. At least this time he wasn't starting from scratch. He knew exactly where she was headed and he could monitor her progress with the GPS tracker on her car.

He sent a text message to Claudia, ignoring the sting of confessing that Autumn had left without him. Claudia would give him grief later, once they prevented a disaster.

Turning on the light he grabbed his jeans from the chair and pulled them on. Finding a shirt, he tugged that over his head, counting all the ways he'd failed Autumn. Unfortunately berating himself didn't get him closer to a solution. What should he have done differently to earn her trust? The entire point in finding her, in working with her, was to make it clear she didn't have to do any of this alone.

When push came to shove, she still ran off to face her demons by herself. He rubbed at the ache behind his sternum. He had to figure out what to change before he found her if this was going to work out.

Or maybe it didn't matter.

Maybe his purpose here was to be a stepping stone, assuming she didn't get killed in her efforts to bring Mosley to justice. Could he be happy knowing he'd helped her through a stage, empowered her to find her happiness somewhere down the line with someone else?

That thought turned the deep ache in his chest to a stabbing pain.

No, life without her wouldn't make him happy at all, unless it was the best thing for her. If so, he'd go back to his solitary life and find a way to deal with her decision. He vowed not to regret a minute with her.

He hadn't expected sex to be enough. A physical connection was a start, but never the entire answer. The part of him aching like a bad tooth decided that opening up and sharing his failures had backfired. It sucked that she didn't see him as a man capable of helping her achieve her primary objective.

She'd left him only one way to prove himself: get over there and intervene. He shoved his phone into his pocket and grabbed his keys hoping like hell he wouldn't be too late.

His heart sank when he stepped outside of the motel. Her car, the one he had tagged with a GPS tracker was still there. Just in case he was dumb enough to think she'd simply taken another vehicle, her scarf was caught in the door. The strip of fabric rippled when the wind caught it as if striving to follow its owner.

Fear caught his neck in a vise and icy fingers danced down his spine. He didn't know how long he stood there unable to move.

Mosley had her. Those three words were on repeat in his head. He couldn't think beyond that simple fact.

Mosley had her.

Now how in the hell was he going to get her back?

Damn. Autumn should've known Tyler was right. Mosley had set another trap and she hadn't just fallen into it, she jumped in with both feet, refusing to listen to reason. Something was *seriously* wrong with her. She supposed that wasn't really news.

It definitely wasn't relevant in the moment.

Two men had jumped her, covering her head with a dark bag and tying her hands before she could begin to fight back. She was furious, mostly with her own blind arrogance.

How had she convinced herself that randomly interfering with Mosley would be effective? His operation was huge and she'd been little more than a lone ant invading his picnic. She'd set out to free the girls and women he still held captive. And when that proved impossible, she'd been sure hauling gangbangers to jail would force him to stop exploiting her Native American sisters.

Somehow she was still a naïve, incurable idealist. Being a captive for an extended period of time had clearly eroded her common sense and emotional stability.

Regrets were useless now. None of the quotes and passages she'd highlighted in the self-help books she'd studied would get her out of *this*. Hell, logic might not be much help in this situation, since logical people didn't go around kidnapping others.

She needed to think like Mosley. He was smart enough to stay a step ahead of the law, but he wasn't infallible. Her escape and continued existence proved that. What did he gain by scooping her up before the planned meeting?

Autumn had been able to pull off the hood and now she tried to think through the rising panic. She needed a strategy and she needed it before Tyler started searching for her. He was a light sleeper and odds were good he'd already realized she was gone. She didn't have much time to take action that would keep him out of harm's way. Being with him had given her such joy, rekindled her belief in happier possibilities, and filled her with hope that she might one day recover from those dreadful years as Mosley's property. Whatever her future held, her life was *not* worth any sacrifice Tyler might be compelled to make.

The hero riding to the rescue was a nice story-line in fairy tales, but she wasn't the sort of princess people loved and celebrated. Nor should they. She was just an angry woman with a wound that she couldn't ignore, bury, or close. When Tyler did something heroic, it should be for a woman who'd earned it.

Thinking about him holding another woman the way he held her brought tears to her eyes. She didn't want to need him so badly, but she had no idea what she'd do when this was done and she had to let him go.

Desperately dragging her thoughts away from that looming abyss, she took a full inventory of her predicament. She wasn't sliding around the back of a pickup truck this time under the hard cover that made it difficult to breathe. She was alone in the back seat of a big sedan that had left its glory somewhere in the 70s. Her hands were tied in front of her with a scratchy rope that chafed her skin. Uncomfortable, but not insurmountable, though she was annoyed that once more she'd have marks on her skin from this group of bottom-feeders. She fought off the swell of anger. Only a clear, sharp mind would get her out of this.

"Thanks for the lift guys," she said, striving for bravado while her mind worked on an effective distraction. "I didn't expect a full escort to my meeting with Mosley today."

"You'll be thanking us all right," the driver said in a menacing growl. His partner in the passenger seat sniggered and the squeaky, nasally sound raked across her nerves like nails on a chalkboard.

With enough time she could get herself untied. But how much time did she have? They weren't taking her to the diner, the town was already well behind them. She didn't want to get caught before she had an escape route figured out. Back when she'd been Mosley's property, she'd seen it happen. Someone would get desperate and bolt without a plan, only to be hauled back and brutally punished to prevent similar attempts.

She peered out into the darkness beyond the car windows, trying to get her bearings. At this hour, when the world was waiting for the first rays of sunlight, it was hard to be sure, but she guessed they were heading west rather than north.

Already clear of town, she'd effectively been wiped off the map. There were no cameras out here for Tyler to pick up the trail. She was on her own. For all she'd told Tyler it was the only way to handle Mosely, fear lifted the hair at the back of her neck. No stores or ranches for miles. No chance of a random witness noticing this car. "It'd be awesome if you could stop for a coffee. A little caffeine would make a world of difference."

"Shut up," the driver snarled. "No one is doing anything you say. Not this time."

"You do realize I *want* to speak with Mosley?" she asked. "I'm not about to bolt now. I've just been short on sleep lately," she said. "Tracking you guys down and calling in tips to the police about your idiotic crimes is a thankless job with late hours."

The driver's furious gaze locked with hers in the rearview mirror. "I said, shut up." He smacked his partner. "Get back there and keep her quiet."

"Why do I gotta do it?" the man complained as he released his seatbelt. "Just turn up the radio or something."

The driver glared at him.

"Fine. But it's not like she can really go anywhere." The muttering was annoying, but better than his icky laughter as he climbed awkwardly over the back of the front seat to join her in the back.

She scooted closer to the door. His breath was stale-beer foul and his long, stringy hair was greasy and held back with a bandana. He reached up and pulled that fabric from his head, wadding it into a ball. "You've done enough talking for one lifetime, missy."

Autumn tried to block him but he caught the rope at her wrists with one hand, holding her arms out of the way as he pressed the gross fabric against her mouth. She clamped her lips together, throwing her head from side to side to avoid the malodorous gag.

"Come on, girl," he said. "It's not like we'll make you wear it the rest of your life." He made that creepy, squeaky sound that passed for laughter right at her ear.

She fought harder, sliding to the floorboard, out of his reach. As she struggled to evade him, they bumped into the back of the driver's seat.

"Get the bitch under control," the driver demanded. "We're almost there."

Autumn couldn't have heard him correctly. What was he talking about? They were in the middle of nowhere. She tucked her knees up and kicked out before Mr. Giggles landed on top of her. The driver turned sharply off the main road, inadvertently helping her as the force pushed Giggles into the back seat.

Her stomach cramped when it dawned on her. These two were likely just the first leg of a transport relay. Those had been prevalent during her captivity. One team picked up the product–drugs, people, or any other contraband–and handed it off for the next leg of the journey. An effective way to compartmentalize information as well as protect the operation as a whole.

They probably weren't taking her directly to Mosely. She didn't have to approve of the tactic to understand what it meant. She had to make a move. The closer she got to Mosley, wherever he was, the more competent and deadly the security would be. She was willing to meet him, on neutral ground and of her own free will, not as a prisoner at a distinct disadvantage. If by some miracle Tyler found her, she didn't want him walking into a deadly ambush.

She scooted backward, over the bump in the floor to the space behind the passenger seat, calculating the man's next attempt to contain her. The driver and his partner argued loudly while she watched the sky grow lighter, considering her options.

It startled her to find comfort in the awareness that Tyler would keep looking for her. After her security detail was compromised before the trial, she'd resisted building connections with people. Everyone she met fell into two categories: a potential threat to her safety or leverage Mosley might use against her. Still, it was pretty clear right now that her plan to wrap this up alone was a big mistake.

What a fine time for *that* epiphany. Tyler would laugh his ass off when she told him, assuming she got the chance. Unlike the ugly Mr. Giggles, Tyler's laughter was deep and warm and thoroughly contagious. Would she ever enjoy that sound sweet, sexy sound again?

Mr. Giggles focused on her again and lunged. She quickly pressed her palms together and swung her hands like an axe, catching him hard across his throat. He sputtered and gurgled and she reared up off the floorboards, shoving him to the far side of the back seat. It gave her just enough time to scramble up onto the seat and throw open the door.

She tumbled out into the road, landing hard. She ignored the pain cascading through her body as she rolled across the pavement and then the biting gravel of the shoulder. Anything was better than going back into Mosley's evil ecosystem.

Resisting help had been a mistake, but from this moment forward she could start making things right.

TYLER COULDN'T WASTE time waiting. He had to find a lead. Whoever Hank or Claudia sent out would need directions and a search area if they were going to find Autumn before something truly awful happened to her.

Again.

His stomach cramped and he shoved away the ugly thoughts that threatened to sidetrack him. He couldn't help her if he was frozen in the what-ifs of Mosley's retaliation and punishment tactics.

Accustomed to using cameras and social media to track people, he was up against it with only one security camera and the trail left behind in the dusty gravel of the motel parking lot.

West was about all he knew. Claudia had delivered two likely places north of town where Mosley might be hiding, but that hardly mattered. Plenty of unmarked north-south routes intersected with that main paved, east-west thoroughfare.

His phone rang and he picked it up. "You've got Tyler."

"Good," a deep voice replied. "This is Bear. Joe Kuntz and his dog Six are with me. Hank Patterson sent us your way."

"I need a tracker with a gift for miracles," Tyler said.

The low rumble on the other end of the call

might have been amusement. "Good thing we're nearly there." Bear verified the address for the motel and promised to be there by first light.

"That's fast work, thanks," Tyler said before ending the call. Relief coursed through him. He hoped like hell Autumn could hang on until they found her.

He consulted state maps and studied the routes on the reservation that were labeled, wishing he had the connections to request a satellite image of the area. What more could he do before Hank's men arrived?

Pray. It was the only thing he hadn't done yet.

He wanted her back so badly, wanted to see her safe and whole. Should he get the chance to hold her again he wouldn't let go. He wouldn't give up on them without a fight. Just imagining her skeptical expression if she heard those words buoyed him in some perverse way.

He understood that she wouldn't tolerate being caught and caged. Not by Tyler or anyone else. That was fine by him. He didn't want to cage her, he only wanted to be her safe haven from the rest of the world. She shouldn't have to feel that hiding was the only way to stay alive or free. Wouldn't it be great if someday her wigs and disguises were just for Halloween?

He scrubbed at his face. She couldn't make any choices about her future until they rescued her from her present dilemma. How could he track her down? West wasn't enough to go on. He drummed his fingers on the map. What would his Guardian Agency bodyguards do in this situation?

First, they'd call him. Since he'd called Claudia, he supposed he was handling the situation correctly. Too bad it didn't move the needle on setting the search parameters. Well, none of the men or women he supported would sit around waiting for help to arrive. They would take some action and let the backup team catch up when they arrived on scene. Tyler could do no less.

He shoved his gun into his waistband and pulled his jacket down over it. If he couldn't follow her with technology he would find another way. Armed with his gun, his cell phone and his map, he marched down to the front office to speak with Debbie and Jeff.

The husband and wife stumbled into the front office together, bleary-eyed at being roused before dawn. "I'm sorry. I know this is inconvenient," Tyler apologized, "but I need a look at the footage from the security camera that monitors the parking lots. Please," he added.

Debbie brought the program online and Tyler

scooted around the desk to join them as they watched the computer monitor. She gasped, and Jeff and Tyler swore when Autumn was grabbed, tied up and tossed into the back seat of an old sedan with a weathered paint job and brand new tires.

"We should call the police," Debbie said.

"I'd rather you didn't," Tyler said. "It could make things worse for her in the short term." Inviting strangers to help him hunt Mosley introduced too many variables and opened up the very real possibility of having someone on Mosley's payroll working against them. He wasn't about to leave the door open for a fox to tear up a henhouse.

"First, I need an expert on the terrain in and around this area," he continued. He spread the map out on the desk. "As you saw, they were heading west out of town."

Debbie and Jeff exchanged a long look. "This is about what Amber is really doing here isn't it?" she asked.

Tyler hesitated, then bobbed his chin. "She's been working against gang activity in the area." Debbie pressed her fingers to her mouth. "We had a meeting set up for tomorrow—today—but as you can see, they got to her first." Again. "Her real name is Autumn Curley," he explained, just in case the reference would sway them to help.

Jeff whistled. "I thought it was her, but she was so guarded and it was obvious she didn't want to be recognized." He rolled his shoulders. "We let her believe we didn't know. More comfortable for all of us."

"I'll make coffee," Debbie volunteered. "Jeff knows the area as well as anyone."

Jeff and Tyler reviewed the maps and vacant places outside of town, including the addresses Claudia suggested. The aroma of fresh brewed coffee filled the small lobby as they discussed likely places to stash a furious and dangerous woman. None of them were west of town.

"You said something about this area?" Jeff tapped the map to the north.

"It's possible that's where Mosley is holed up, calling the shots," Tyler replied. "I just don't know for sure. It gives him a pretty clean route to and from the diner where we were supposed to meet."

"*Hm.* Not much out that way past the creek."

"If anyone can navigate on not much, it's Autumn," Tyler said.

"True. The Curley family is known for their tracking skills, going back generations. Long before anyone bothered with written records and newcomers changed the landscape around here." Jeff dragged a finger along the jagged trail of the creek. "If Mosley really is up here, heading west is a big waste of time."

"Why?"

"It's nothing but grassland or barren, cracked dirt between here and there." Jeff scowled. "Hard country to cross in the vehicle they were driving." Debbie returned with coffee and Jeff took the offered cup with a soft word of thanks.

That understated closeness, the innate partnership was an intimacy more important to Tyler than sex. It was love, pure and glowing in each simple, caring action. Autumn deserved a chance at that solid kind of life, even if it wasn't with him.

Tyler watched Jeff's finger slide over the map. "In that car, there's no way they can get from this road to that location."

He'd have to call Claudia. "They must have another vehicle waiting out there, one better suited to the task," Tyler murmured. That explained the logistics, but not the reason for going so far out of their way.

"Or they aren't taking her to the location you think," Debbie said. Tyler and Jeff stared at her. "Amber—Autumn—has caused the gang in this particular area a ton of grief. Honestly, I'm surprised it took anyone this long to connect the blond bombshell to the mysterious tips and hog tied criminals dumped at police stations." Debbie *tsked*, shaking her head. "Far as I know the tribal police didn't look too hard for the ghost deputy dragging in bad guys."

"I agree, but Mosley has been looking for her since he found a way to compromise the secure witness locations before the trial last year," Tyler said.

Jeff swore. "She's embarrassed him time and again. First escaping, giving an airtight testimony, and punching holes in his operation all over the area. He doesn't want a meeting, he wants to make her an example."

Debbie looked at the map and back at the video showing taillights of the car leaving the parking lot. "No," she whispered. Her hands clutched her mug, her knuckles white.

Tyler's skin went cold all over and then prickled with a rash of heat. "What do you mean?"

"Historically, tribes employed cruel, slow methods of torture for prisoners. They had specific ways to dispense with an offender or enemy that ensured lengthy public suffering that fit the crime."

Tyler could barely find his voice. "You think he's planning a public punishment for Autumn?"

Jeff rubbed his eyes. "I don't want to think about it, but it adds up. Mosley has lost key members of his gangs thanks to her. His closest people must be doubting his ability to keep the money flowing. Hell, with the way she's been picking off his low- and mid-level crews, the gangs would be more likely to follow her. Power and strength matter."

"But this is the twenty-first century," Tyler protested. He couldn't fathom what Jeff was implying.

"The Native Mob is ruthless," Debbie whispered as if speaking the words loudly would bring the operation right into her lobby. "Jeff's right. They'll make an example of her. Killing her fast or humanely doesn't serve any purpose. Plus, if you head almost due west, you pass a traditional site where the Crow Indians dealt out punishment."

Jeff swore. "She's right. I forgot about that. They would stake out offenders to bake in the sun, leaving the remains for vultures and scavengers."

Tyler's stomach pitched. "You're serious." The thought of Autumn enduring more suffering at the hands of Mosley had him wanting to light the entire state on fire. "Since the moment this case hit

my desk I've heard about the reach of and ruthless-
ness of the Native Mob. Autumn was right, this
bastard must be eliminated."

"I'll pretend I didn't hear that." A deep, rusty
voice had them all turning toward the door.

Tyler blanched. The man wasn't wearing a local
law enforcement uniform, but he carried himself
with unarguable authority: bad guys beware. The
big German shepherd at his side only added to the
intimidation factor.

"Excuse us," Debbie stepped forward. "I'm
afraid we didn't hear the bell. How can we help?"

The man tipped his head toward Tyler. "We're
here to help him."

It clicked for Tyler in that instant. "Hank
Patterson sent you, right?" He started forward,
stopping when the dog's ears perked and the intelligent, assessing gaze locked onto him.

"That's right. I'm Joe Kuntz." He tipped his head
to the dog. "And this is Six."

"It's good to meet you," Tyler said without
moving. "Debbie and Jeff own the motel. Mr.
Kuntz and Six helped us find Autumn's sister when
one of the Native Mob assassin's caught up with
her."

"Call me Joe." He gave them a faint smile. "Bear
will join us in a minute. Had to take a call. Then we

can roll out." He cocked an eyebrow and Tyler would've sworn his dog did the same. "Assuming you know where we're headed."

"You got here fast."

"Hank stationed us close when he heard what you were working on. Found your lost witness, huh?"

"Yes. And everything indicates I underestimated the man hunting her."

"Happens to the best of us," Joe said. A bigger man walked in and the lobby was suddenly way too small. "Bear," Joe said as an introduction. "Debbie, Joe, and Tyler."

"No kidding." Bear stared at Tyler. "You're not what I pictured after all those phone calls."

"Yeah, I look different when I'm not behind a computer," Tyler said. "Claudia and Hank filled you in?"

"They did," Bear confirmed. "Anything new?"

"Debbie thinks she knows where they're taking Autumn," Tyler replied. Could he repeat the theory without losing his cool?

"Let me hear it," Bear said, striding up to the desk. "I'm not as good as the famous Curley trackers, but I'm no slouch." He kept his eyes on the map while Tyler, Jeff and Debbie took turns filling him in. "Not much cover out that way," he said.

"Then we'd better work on approach options on the way," Joe interjected. "If we wait much longer, we'll lose any element of surprise with the sunrise."

With a thanks to the motel owners, Tyler followed the men and dog to a dark pickup truck. Bear hopped up into the driver's seat and Joe climbed into the back of the crew cab with Six, leaving the front passenger seat for Tyler.

"I didn't want to say it in there," Bear began, "But Hank is following Claudia's research to Mosley's likely hideout. Colin and Dallas are with him."

"Mosley is more likely to be wherever Autumn is," Tyler said.

"Sure," Bear agreed. "Which is why we're armed to the teeth with weapons, Six, and radios. My call was to the tribal police, letting them know we're here searching for a friend who has disappeared."

"Do you expect them to join the search?" Tyler asked, concerned and aggravated that Autumn would be exposed one way or another by the time this was over. She deserved better than to have her private life blasted out through official reports and any resulting media.

He swallowed an ugly outburst. These men were here to help. He should be aiming that frustration at himself. By tracking her down and trying to save the day, he'd compounded the trouble for her. Feeling cornered, she'd reacted accordingly.

"They're welcome to try," Joe said as Bear sped down the open road. "We didn't give them the most accurate starting point."

"You didn't?" Tyler felt small and insignificant next to this team. Even Six had a big presence that oozed confidence. Tyler was fit, but he was much stronger and felt far more effective with his computer.

"Hell no," Bear scoffed. "We remember the nightmare of this case when communication was compromised. The fewer people who know where we're going, the better."

"But Debbie and Jeff know," he said, thinking out loud. "She wanted to call the police."

"I doubt there's anyone at the station to take her call right now," Joe said. "Besides, we have a head start and the best tracker in the region, aside from the woman we're tracking."

Tyler hoped that would be enough to get them to Autumn before Mosley did something they couldn't overcome.

∾

AUTUMN WAS face down in the dirt on the far side of the ditch when her body stopped moving. Grass tickled her cheek and she felt loose and weak as a ragdoll caught up in a strong wind. Her ribs burned and every nerve in her body was screaming in protest. In the risky escape, she lost track of sounds. It was a miracle she hadn't lost consciousness. Had the driver stopped yet? She didn't hear any motors from the road and she couldn't imagine him driving on to the destination without her. Letting down Mosley was as good as suicide. Rolling to her back, she stared up at the softness in the sky. A fresh day would be here soon and if she didn't find cover, she'd be easy picking.

She sipped a shallow, measured breath, taking stock of her surroundings. The ground at her back was cool, the tall, spiky grass not nearly tall enough to be good cover. The good news was that the rope binding her wrists had snapped during her tumble.

"Over here!" came the shout from the road.

That was the driver, not Mr. Giggles. Time to move. On her belly, she crawled away from the road, praying she'd find a place to hide before they noticed her.

The rattle of dirt and loose stones, rushing footsteps followed her. They were too close and she was in no condition to outrun two men. Then again, she'd rather be dead than walk willingly into whatever horrors Mosley wanted to inflict on her.

The way they'd spoken to her in the car, she had a good idea of the fate Mosley had planned for her. She remembered the stories and dark, ghastly history of the landmark nearby. Her grandfather had walked this way with her as a child, telling her tales of bravery and cowardice. There were stories of ceremonies and challenges too, personal rites of passage that were designed to cleanse the mind and body to make a warrior worthy, strong, and honorable.

Mosley and his gangs had nothing honorable in mind for her.

She found it easier to breathe with every passing minute, but she felt them gaining on her. She wouldn't meet them on her belly or her knees. She would stand and fight. Out in this stretch of the reservation running for help was an exercise in futility. Two men had the clear advantage against one average-sized woman. Still, better to face two enemies here than whatever number waited for her at their intended destination.

Crouching low, she studied the landscape to get her bearings and a feel for how much space remained between her and the men. Stars danced in front of her eyes for a moment and blood dripped from her chin.

"I found the bitch!" Giggles shrieked. He hopped up and down. "Get over here now!"

She wasn't sure if he was talking to her or the driver. Didn't really matter. Both men were only a few yards away. Giggles stayed in front of her while the driver moved to flank her.

"Good to see you too," she said through clenched teeth. "Any chance I can convince you to tell him I died on the way?"

The driver's gaze narrowed, sliding over her from head to toe. "I don't get paid to deliver you dead or damaged."

"He wants you all fancied up," Giggles added. "Before he kills you slowly."

Somehow knowing what they meant without having it all spelled out was more terrifying than if they'd simply listed the order of humiliating, gruesome, and unbearable events she could expect in the coming hours.

Head down, doing her best to appear defeated, she moved toward Giggles. He was smaller and, sporting the marks of her previous attack, he was a little scared of her. There would be another opening, another chance to get away. She had to keep believing that survival was possible. Just as she'd done the first time she'd been kidnapped and dragged into Mosley's criminal enterprises.

The driver rushed her from behind, apparently wanting to urge her closer to Giggles and the road. Instead of fighting back, she pretended to collapse from the impact. Unfortunately, there wasn't much acting required. She pitched forward, tucked into a ball and rolled to her feet, his gun in her hand. She fired a single shot into the air and as a cloud of birds took to the sky, she ran, legs churning through the thick grasses and weeds, praying she wouldn't twist an ankle in a hole or trip over a random clod of dirt.

The reality was worse. She ran right off the edge of a break in the meadow and was once again tumbling, at the mercy of gravity and the unforgiving terrain. At least this time, the men didn't follow her.

She heard their raised voices overhead. They couldn't see her, tucked under the outcropping she'd fallen over. Frustrated, neither of them followed her down. After a short discussion, the voices faded to silence. She assumed they'd left to meet Mosley and report the situation so they could bring back reinforcements to search for her.

She had to make the most of the small window of opportunity. Checking the loaded gun, she slowly crept away, aiming for the last place anyone would expect her to go: straight for the ceremonial ground. It would be a hike over rugged terrain, but she could cut the angle and follow the creek. With a little luck, she'd find the bastard and put an end to his reign today.

CHAPTER 12

Bear pulled over when he his headlights caught on skid marks that ended in the gravel on the shoulder. "This could be something. Looks fresh."

Please let it be a clue, Tyler thought as they all piled out of the truck. Six put his nose to the ground, immediately catching something of interest. They followed the dog around a disturbance in the gravel, flattened grass at the edge of a ditch and a small bit of rope.

"Looks like she's free," Joe said.

"Lots of fresh action here," Bear added. He looked up and down the stretch of deserted roadway. "They must have left."

"With or without her?" Tyler wondered, studying the length of rough rope. The knot had held but the restraint had snapped in the middle. At the deepest part of the ditch Six skidded to a stop and whined. The crushed grass created a path away from the road and it was easy to assume someone had crawled through recently, staying low.

Joe praised Six and gave him the signal to keep searching.

"Not much blood," Bear pointed out as he crouched near a small dark spot in the grass. He eyed Tyler. "Maybe she jumped from the moving car and skinned something up."

Definitely something Autumn would attempt. Not much blood was good news and her hands were free. In his mind that added up to her still being free. But if so, where was she now? "Tied up or not, it doesn't surprise me that she found a way to get out of the car."

"Assuming this is her blood, the trail is easier to follow," Joe said, moving further from the road with Six in the lead.

Which was a subtle way of pointing out that the men who'd taken her from the motel could've found her and taken her away. "How many other people would be out here causing trouble and leaving a blood trail this morning?" Tyler asked.

He didn't get an answer from Bear or Joe, just

the dog's deep bark carrying through the early morning quiet. "Six is onto something."

They all jogged to catch up with him. Joe got there first, Tyler on his heels. Flanking the dog, they peered over the side of a washout. Something, or someone had tumbled down. "Would've been too dark to see this ten minutes ago," Joe said. "First step would've been a shock."

"Looks like signs of a struggle a few yards back," Bear said, joining them. "If it was Autumn, she might've made a stand and managed to escape."

"Escape right over a cliff," Tyler said. He pushed his hands through his hair and swore.

Bear leaned over the edge and cast his flashlight around. "Cliff? Hardly." He crouched down, favoring a knee. "I agree with Six that this is our trail. Best if we keep going."

They clambered down, mindful of the loose dirt. "Here we go." Bear ducked into a hollow made by the washout. "Perfect cover."

Tyler looked around for any sign or clue from Autumn. Six, snuffling the area and eager to follow the scent was their only confirmation she'd been here. He scolded himself for feeling hurt that she hadn't left him some kind of message. Autumn would've been caught by the wrong people long

"Trail ends here," Joe said. "She must have gone into the creek."

Bear agreed after wandering a few paces up and down the creek. "I don't see a good crossing place."

"I don't think she crossed." Obstacles meant nothing to Autumn when she was working against Mosley's gangs. Tyler pulled out his phone, using the GPS app to pinpoint their current location. "If she went into the creek, it's because she thinks she can ambush Mosley."

Joe's mouth fell open. "You're serious."

Tyler nodded, sliding his phone into the inner pocket of his jacket and drawing his gun. "She was inside his operation for a long time. She knows how things work. Mosley expected his men to deliver. Most likely she's counting on him coming out to punish them personally for losing her." He pointed in the general direction of Mosley's suspected hideout, and then toward the ceremonial ground Debbie mentioned. "On the map, there's a bridge about a mile up that crosses this creek. It's the most direct route between the two locations."

"Pissed off and convinced he's the top dog, he won't bother with an indirect path," Bear mused.

"That was my thought."

They hadn't gone much further when the

sound of gunfire sailed over the wispy fog clinging to the creek bank. Men and dog froze and Bear got on the radio to give Hank a status update.

The few seconds felt like hours to Tyler before the radio crackled and a reply came back. "Hold your position," Hank said. "Claudia pinged a cell phone and we were rolling up to that location when gunfire broke out. I can see an SUV blocking a bridge over the creek. Not sure if the driver is stuck or making a barricade. A smaller car is wedged in behind it. We're hanging back for now."

Hearing that report, Tyler charged forward, heedless of what Bear and Joe and Hank might decide to do. He had to give Autumn an assist. She'd handled too much of this mess on her own, too afraid to believe anyone would stand with her against the powerful crime boss.

Love and desperation churned through him as he sprinted, following the creek around a bend and through a stand of trees. As he broke into the clearing, the scene looked and sounded more like a war than a skirmish between members of the same gang.

Then he saw her, only a few more yards ahead, close to the low bridge. His heart skipped, stuttered.

She stood like a goddess of vengeance rising

from the waters of the rushing creek. Tyler recognized Mosley's preferred matte black SUV leaning precariously at the edge of the bridge. It looked as if it would fall into the creek at any moment.

The drop wouldn't be enough to kill anyone in the car, unless they got pinned and the creek drowned them before they could get out. A man could hope.

"Autumn!" he shouted in vain. She couldn't possibly hear him over the water and the engine revving uselessly.

To his left he saw a silver pickup truck blocking the road with the help of a sheriff's SUV. Three men, weapons drawn, were using it for cover. He recognized Hank, Colin, and Dallas, ready to intervene at the first opportunity.

Whoever was inside the vehicle might still escape if they could get out and make a run back toward the house. Someone needed to flank the SUV. Someone other than Tyler. No way would he leave Autumn's side.

The black muzzle of a gun poked through a broken window in the SUV and Tyler saw the flare a moment before he heard the shot aimed at him.

He threw himself to the ground and returned fire.

Autumn spun around, saw him, and grinned.

She was amazing. It was the most beautiful sight, better than any sunrise after a bad nightmare. Water flew from her loose hair as she turned back and fired a gun at the SUV. The vehicle lurched as a tire went flat. That lurch saved his hide from a bullet as the shooter's aim was thrown off by the unexpected shift.

She must have taken the gun from the men who'd caught her and this time she aimed at the exposed gas tank. From his vantage point, Tyler saw Bear, Joe and Six moving closer to pin down Mosley and his crew. They could be seriously injured if she fired now.

Tyler darted into the creek and bumped Autumn under the shelter of the bridge.

"I had the shot!" she wailed. "Mosley is in the SUV."

She'd been willing to kill the man. He wasn't surprised and he couldn't blame her. He wanted Mosley dead too. "He won't be for long," Tyler said, holding her close. "The good guys have him surrounded."

"They do?" She wiped her damp face with the back of her hand.

"Yes. Colin, Dallas, the sheriff, Hank Patterson—"

"Who?" She leaned back, her face flushed with adrenaline, her dark eyes sparkling.

"Doesn't matter." He tucked a lock of her wet hair behind her ear. "I was so damned worried."

Overhead the vehicle creaked ominously, metal frame scraping against the bridge rail. He eyed the structure and decided it was best to wait right here until he got the all clear.

"Are you hurt?" He examined a deep scrape along her brow bone. Found another scrape under her torn sleeve. "Well, this explains the blood we found."

"You were looking for me."

"Hell, yes," he replied though it wasn't really a question. He lifted her hands so he could press gentle kisses to the abrasions at her wrists where she'd been tied. Suddenly a dog was barking up on the road. "That's Six, K9 partner to one of Hank's men."

"Again, Hank who?"

"He leads the Brotherhood Protectors, the company who helped my teams find Marnie and Summer. You'll meet them all soon enough."

She shied away at that statement, but he only hauled her back into another hug. Overhead, the guardrail failed and he heard screams as the vehicle dropped into the creek. The impact rumbled under their feet. He put his body between the SUV and her, eager to get her out of this cold water. "Later I want to hear how you got out of that car."

Behind them and up on the road, more shouts followed as everyone closed in on Mosley and his men.

"You crazy bitch!" Mosley's shriek startled them both.

Autumn went rigid in Tyler's arms, then twisted away, raising her gun. He was a beat slower, but pulled the trigger as soon as he saw the bastard take aim at her. More gunshots rang out from the road, the sounds echoing off the cement of the bridge and ringing in his ears, a violent symphony as bullets tore through the water.

Mosley fell backward into the creek and the current swept his blood downstream, away from Autumn.

It would take a full forensics investigation to sort out which of them fired the fatal shot, if anyone even bothered. Tyler thought not knowing was the best possible outcome, especially for Autumn. She didn't need that additional burden, though he knew she'd been more than ready to carry it.

He turned her away as the authorities waded into the creek to recover the body.

"You planning on swimming forever?" Bear was crouched on the bank, blankets in hand. One of the paramedics on scene was reaching out a hand to help them up.

"Come on," he said to Autumn. "Let's get you dried off and warm."

She nodded, her teeth starting to chatter. "That's all you have to say?" she asked, reaching for the paramedic's hand.

"Not even close," Tyler replied. He had plenty to say, but the personal declarations had to wait for all the official statements to be completed.

And he didn't want an audience for the conversation they really needed to have. He'd start with an overdue 'I love you' and see where that led. He wanted more, forever really, but he couldn't force his needs on her. She had loads of healing ahead of her, he could only hope she'd let him stick around and support her though it all.

Autumn thought the day would never end. She answered questions while her skin prickled all over. The cold creek was only one cause. The sheer number of eyes on her, seeing her and listening was dreadfully uncomfortable. If Tyler had walked away she never would've gotten through all the explanations.

The whole thing sounded crazy in her ears and she'd lived it. She'd delivered petty criminals to the tribal police station. She and Tyler had stopped a kidnapping attempt. And she had managed to escape yet another trap and bring Mosley down. The human trafficking ring plaguing this region was now closed.

The chief from the tribal police department stood with the sheriff, the men working together to take her statement so she wouldn't have to endure all of this a second time.

Tyler turned away at one point to speak quietly with the man he introduced as Hank Patterson, but he'd held on to her hand the entire time.

She'd told herself she'd never be tied down to any man, never let herself lean or depend on anyone for her safety. It had been her one sure plan before Tyler had walked into the Wild Bee. Although she didn't want to admit it, over the past several days he'd changed everything, including her theory that she didn't need anyone.

She glanced at him from the corner of her eye when the questions were finally done. Mosley's body had been recovered and transported in a coroner's van. A few of the men who had helped Tyler had left, including a dog that had taken down one of the thugs loyal to Mosley. Oh how she wished she'd seen that in person.

Two men remained, a redhead and a man with Native American heritage. At the moment they were leaning against a pickup truck, dark sunglasses shielding their eyes. She hadn't been introduced, but they must be the men who had rescued her sister and Marnie.

Tyler had told her that both Marnie and Summer were fine, but seeing the men who'd made that possible somehow brought it all home for her.

"All right," the chief of the tribal police department said. "You two can go, but you'll need to stay close in case we have follow up questions."

"No," Tyler countered. "You can't ask us to stay in this area. Everyone has seen her face, they know who she really is."

The older man's eyes narrowed. "They know to leave this woman and all her family alone. I have patrols at your father's place," he said to Autumn. "If you want to go home, it's safe to do so."

Did she want that?

The sheriff cleared his throat. "Autumn,

according to your statement, Mosley planned a public humiliation and execution to send a message." He paused, waiting for her to meet his gaze. "Instead, you've delivered a message of your own. If you were a rival, you would control the mob now. Retaliation isn't a true concern."

Maybe not today, but what about tomorrow? In time, someone else would rise to lead the Native Mob and greed and power trips would override common sense again. The cycle made her queasy.

"He's right," Tyler said in his quiet way. He didn't try to hold her, only remained within her reach in case she needed him. She would miss that if she retreated into herself again. "They might be angry, but no one else has any reason to come after you."

Sincerity glowed in his eyes. Wouldn't it be nice if she could believe as easily as he did? The world wasn't a nice place and she'd been stuck in one of the most depraved corners. "I hope you're right." It was too late now, too many people had seen her and would know where to start if they wanted to track her down. Her lingering fears, rational or not, weren't Tyler's to resolve. That was on her.

"Come on," he said. "Colin and Dallas can give us a ride back to the motel." There was a sadness in his smile. "Then you can pack up and I'll take you wherever you want to go."

Was there anything she still wanted at the motel room? She supposed they could discuss it once they were alone. If she was lucky, Tyler would be a willing sounding board one more time.

On the drive back to the motel, Colin explained how he'd met her sister, Summer. "She'd like to see you, whenever you feel ready."

Autumn reached for Tyler's hand, gripping hard so her voice wouldn't shake. "I'm not sure." All this talk of a wispy, undefined future left her jumpy.

"No one will rush you," Tyler promised.

"Can I tell Marnie you're all right?" Dallas asked. "Eagle Rock is one of the best small towns around," he added. "Everyone who was in the cafe the day you escaped wants to know you're okay."

While they'd been working together, Tyler had mentioned Dallas's family ties to the reservations and how upset he'd been to learn the Native Mob were stealing and selling their own women and girls like cattle.

Colin shifted in the seat, removing his sunglasses. "We don't know what you endured. Don't need to know anything unless you want to share. But everyone aware of this case considers you a hero."

He probably meant the words to be a comfort, but they stung her skin like an icy wind. She'd simply done what was necessary to survive. It only looked like she'd gone above and beyond because her actions were so far outside the logic most people recognized.

Tyler had scooted closer to her on the back seat. Or maybe she'd scooted up to him. Either way, she appreciated his support and the quiet steadiness that never seemed to wane.

"Tyler said Marnie returned to Eagle Rock." she said.

Dallas nodded. "Still keeping people in pie at the cafe."

That made her heart happy. She looked at Colin, her brother-in-law again. "And where do you and Summer live?"

"We're mobile right now," Colin replied. "Based in Colorado. She's sorting out how she wants to get back into teaching. If she does."

"She's an excellent teacher," Autumn said. "Anyone who can make math interesting should keep at it."

Colin chuckled. "I'll tell her you said so. Just

remember that we can come to you, if that's better when the time is right."

Dallas turned into the motel parking lot and pulled to a stop in front of the office. Debbie and Jeff rushed out to greet them, relief and worry stamped on their faces. She wondered who had told them she was coming.

"Thank you both," Autumn said. "Tyler can help me get in contact when I've made some decisions."

She was barely out of the car before Debbie was hugging her. Instead of cringing and retreating, she actually laughed at the affectionate display and hugged the other woman, her first friend since the ordeal. She let Tyler handle the brief explanations about the events leading up to Mosley's death and then they excused themselves.

In her motel room, finally alone, she didn't know where to start. He'd nudged her into the shower and told her to use up all the hot water. Once they were both in fresh clothes and feeling normal, she let her mind mull where she should go next. Was there a place that felt like home anymore?

Packing wasn't an issue, she just didn't know where to take the few items she counted as both hers and necessary. What did she do with herself now that Mosley had been stopped?

At the table, Tyler was stowing his computer and accessories into the travel bag. Giving her space, making no demands. Suddenly it infuriated her. If he really cared so damn much, shouldn't he want something from her for himself?

"What are you doing?" she snapped, hating the way her voice squeaked. He couldn't be her sole source of strength. "I'll never go back to being a voiceless, cooperative wimp."

"Wimp?" He rolled his eyes. "You've got your terms crossed."

She gasped. "I said that out loud?"

"You did."

She slumped to the bed and covered her face with her hands. All the fight drained out of her as fast as it had filled her. "Sorry."

"Don't be. Just my opinion, but you haven't let yourself feel or react to anything in far too long." Clearly he was forgetting just how much feeling and reacting she'd done while they made love. She would miss that if they parted ways, but she wasn't sure it was fair to him if she didn't go her own way.

"I don't know what I want," she confessed behind her hands. "Confused." Tears were close and whether they flowed from adrenaline, fear, or outright anguish, she didn't want to cry. Not over the innocence and dreams she'd lost to the mob's system.

"Can I tell you what I want?" he asked.

She dropped her hands to her lap. "Please."

He knelt in front of her, his hands to either side of her knees, but he didn't touch her. "I want you to be happy. However long that takes, wherever that journey takes you, I want you happy."

"That's cheating, Ty." She curled her fingers around his wrists and just explored the strength in the man's warm hands. He'd taken a life today, or part of one, in defense of her. He'd seen things she couldn't imagine, experienced grief she wasn't sure she could bear in his place. But he could smile, he could kiss, and he could laugh. He had nightmares, but he kept moving forward, searching and finding a new place, a new purpose. "What do you want for *you*? For your life?"

"You were always more than a cold case, Autumn. I'm satisfied you're out of danger and that's a big win for me as well as the Guardian Agency."

He closed his eyes and when he opened them, there were no more secrets, no more veiled emotions. She saw more love and acceptance in his blue gaze than she'd ever seen before.

"I love you," he said. "What I want more than

anything is to have you with me. I want to be your happy place, your partner through every day ahead of us, good or bad. And I know that what I want is something I can't ask for. I won't."

"Ask."

"No, Autumn. I love you. I want you to hear that, to feel it and soak it in without any ties or pressure."

Reaching out, she ran her fingertips over the stubble of his whiskers. He would let her walk away, though she sincerely doubted he would stop keeping an eye on her. "Is your life very public?"

"Are you kidding?" He laughed. "My career is almost always behind the scenes. Today was the first time I'd seen Colin and Dallas in person. My mentor at the agency is a woman I've only spoken with by phone or text. Agency personnel are scattered all over the country. Company picnics and holiday parties aren't really the GA style."

"So if you had a partner, she wouldn't have to play hostess for your boss or anything?"

"What is this 1950? No, of course not."

"And if you had a partner, would she be responsible for fixing dinner and stuff like that?"

"You want to know about the partner of my dreams?"

She nodded, needing his answer more than she needed her next breath.

Slowly, giving her ample time to move, he came close enough to touch his nose to hers. "The woman I want to call mine for the rest of my days has mad bartending skills. I'd only ask that she fix the drinks in the relationship. Everything else is negotiable, day by day."

"Everything else?" Her lips feathered over his and then she was finally kissing him properly. Deeply, letting love vanquish every vulnerability. When she eased back, her heart pounding and her hands linked behind his neck, she knew what she wanted. What she couldn't live without. This man. She had a ways to go and there would be hard days ahead of them, but she couldn't picture a content life that didn't include him. If he wouldn't ask her, she would just have to do it.

"I love you, Tyler." It was a struggle to hold his gaze, a new sensation to willingly let another person see her so unguarded. His palms pressed into her hips, tender and possessive in the most protective way. "Will you be my love, my anchor, and my partner for the rest of our days? Wherever you are is the only place my heart can call home."

"Autumn." He claimed her mouth, set her blood on fire. "Yes, absolutely yes." He whispered the word over and over across her cheeks, her ear, her jaw and back to her mouth. "You've made me the happiest man on the planet."

"You mean it," she murmured, a little awestruck. She didn't deserve a man this good, yet she was done trying to peel off the sticky shadows of fear, humiliation, and pain by herself.

"I do."

Her heart lifted, took flight. She was free and safe and home at last. It wouldn't be easy to trust in all this goodness or look straight at the bright light of happiness, but with Tyler, she could see the glimmer of a rainbow in her future and the solid foundation under her feet.

"Then we should probably figure out what comes next." She bounced a little on the bed. "You probably noticed I'm not the greatest at people-ing anymore."

"You'll get there when you're ready." He had such confidence. "But maybe a trip to Disney World should wait a while."

She thumped him on the arm, hiding how the mere suggestion made her tremble. He just kissed her again.

"I don't even know where you live." She flung an arm toward her duffle bag and backpack. "Is there room for my stuff at your place?"

He laughed. Standing up, he plucked her into his arms and spun her in a circle. "There will always be room for you and your stuff in my life. I love you, Autumn Curley."

"I love you too." Now that she'd said it she didn't want to stop. "I'd like to see my sister and Marnie, but maybe not right away."

"No one set any kind of a timer. But you might like Eagle Rock. Small town, friendly faces, lots of protective people and loads of wide open spaces."

She nibbled on her lip, thinking. "It made me feel safe enough to take a chance that day," she said. "Could we drive through?"

"Whatever you need, we can do," he vowed.

Right now, she needed him and his open acceptance more than anything else.

EPILOGUE

AFTER ONE LAST night at the motel, Autumn was ready to leave. Debbie and Jeff were as stunned as Tyler when she handed Jeff the keys to her car and left the wigs and clothing for Debbie to share as she saw fit. Her knives and gun came along with them. No surprise there. She wouldn't part with the weapons until she was ready, but he counted it a step in the right direction when she slipped her mother's necklace over her head.

Every small victory mattered and Tyler was sure that gesture meant she felt hope that one day she could reconnect with her family.

In Eagle Rock, he cruised down the center of town, passing the diner and the other shops along the main street. She didn't fidget, but her eyes were wide as she took it all in. She didn't want to stop either, so they kept going without a word to anyone.

Only Hank knew they were in the area. Thanks to the former SEAL's many connections, Tyler found a rental cabin on a ranch that had been converted into a tourist property. He'd spoken with Swann and was officially back on the tech support roster, with a raise and a commendation in his file. Apparently helping Autumn flush out Mosley and bust up the Native Mob had been cause for serious celebration in the federal prosecutor's office.

After a few days he and Autumn settled into a comfortable routine. Long walks together within the shelter of the Crazy Mountains gave her time to unload or just rest in quiet companionship. She explored online options for various college programs while he worked and she spent as much time outside as possible. Resting, healing, and discovering who she wanted to be. At night they made love and slept with a peace and contentment that was long overdue for both of them.

He didn't press, didn't expose her location, not even when Colin inquired on behalf of Summer. When Autumn was ready, they would take the next step.

So it was a surprise when she invited him out on a date to Marnie's cafe for coffee and pie.

As if that wasn't enough of a shock, when they reached the cafe, there was a closed sign on the door. "Marnie did that for me," Autumn explained.

"Baby steps?" he queried.

"Pretty much." She gave his hand a hard squeeze before they walked up to the door. "And Dallas is here. I hope you don't mind a private double date kind of deal."

"It'll be great." He wanted her to get out and explore being normal, but he never wanted her to push herself too fast. She'd done enough pushing for one lifetime.

Marnie greeted them, Dallas just behind her.

When the door was locked again, the four of them headed for the long counter, away from the front windows. "You're doing great," he said.

"*Mm-hm.*"

The couples chatted while Marnie served coffee. He noticed there were two more thick white mugs set out and he hoped that meant Summer and Colin were also invited.

He was thrilled when they all turned at the sound of a knock at the door. For the longest moment it seemed the sisters could only stare at each other, frozen in place on either side of the glass.

Then Marnie opened the door and they were hugging and crying and talking over each other. Tears of joy, he hoped. Words of love and comfort too. The Curley family didn't need any more sorrow.

Summer dried her cheeks and gave Autumn a watery smile. "I thought you'd never call. I don't mean that as judgement."

"I didn't take it that way," Autumn said immediately. "You look wonderful, by the way."

"Thanks." She twisted a tissue in her hands. "Dad's in the car. Just in case you want to see him. If you don't, if you're not ready..." Her voice trailed off as Autumn shot out of the cafe toward Summer's car.

Tyler watched through the window, floored and amazed at how easily Autumn was managing the unexpected.

"She looks amazing and healthy," Summer said. "Thank you."

Tyler waved off the praise. "It's all her," he said. "She just needed time to remember the world still has more good stuff going on than bad."

"You're a good man, Tyler," Marnie said.

"Without you, I'm not sure any of us would've found our way home."

"You're embarrassing him," Colin pointed out. "I like it." He and Dallas laughed as Autumn and Mr. Curley walked into the cafe.

Marnie flipped the lock on the front door and shooed them all to the back counter where she had several pies ready to serve. She cut thick slices of cherry pie for Tyler and Dallas and Summer, apple for herself, and chocolate silk for Colin, Autumn, and Mr. Curley. It delighted Tyler to see Autumn indulging herself.

It was strange hanging out with the bodyguards he wasn't actually supposed to meet face to face. And though he was curious about Dallas's background and Colin's story, he wouldn't wreck a good thing by snooping. That would be a breach of his contract. Swann was probably having a conniption fit over the rather fluid state of the usual anonymity and isolation protocols. He'd get over it.

This case had been unique from the start and now, when these three men from the Guardian Agency headed to their respective homes, it would be with happiness and contentment to balance the grit and courage and unflagging determination essential to maintaining a high agency success rate and excellent client satisfaction.

"What are you thinking about?" Autumn asked him as the others were caught up in a discussion of an upcoming summer movie.

"You," he said, giving her hand a squeeze under the table. "And what a difference love makes."

The End

ABOUT THE AUTHOR

Regan Black, a USA Today and internationally bestselling author, writes award-winning, action-packed romances featuring kick-butt heroines and the sexy heroes who fall in love with them. Raised in the Midwest and California, she and her husband enjoy an empty-nest life in the South Carolina Lowcountry where the rich blend of legend, romance, and history fuels her imagination.

For book news and special offers, subscribe to Regan's newsletter.

Keep up with Regan online:
www.ReganBlack.com
Follow Regan on Amazon
Follow Regan on BookBub
Facebook Reader Group

BROTHERHOOD PROTECTORS WORLD

ORIGINAL SERIES BY ELLE JAMES

Brotherhood Protectors Hawaii World

Team Koa Alpha

Lane Unleashed - Regan Black

Harlan Unleashed - Stacey Wilk

Raider Unleashed - Lori Matthews

Waylen Unleashed - Jen Talty

Kian Unleashed - Kris Norris

Brotherhood Protectors Yellowstone World

Team Wolf

Guarding Harper - - Desiree Holt

Guarding Hannah - Delilah Devlin

Guarding Eris - Reina Torres

Guarding Payton - Jen Talty

Guarding Leah - Regan Black

Team Eagle

Booker's Mission - Kris Norris

Hunter's Mission - Kendall Talbot

Gunn's Mission - Delilah Devlin

Xavier's Mission - Lori Matthews

Wyatt's Mission - Jen Talty

Corbin's Mission - Jen Talty

Tyson's Mission - Delilah Devlin

Knox's Mission - Barb Han

Colton's Mission - Kendall Talbot

Walker's Mission - Kris Norris

Brotherhood Protectors Colorado World
Team Watchdog

Mason's Watch - Jen Talty

Asher's Watch - Leanne Tyler

Cruz's Watch - Stacey Wilk

Kent's Watch- Deanna L. Rowley

Ryder's Watch- Kris Norris

Team Raptor

Darius' Promise - Jen Talty

Simon's Promise - Leanne Tyler

Nash's Promise - Stacey Wilk

Spencer's Promise - Deanna L. Rowley

Logan's Promise - Kris Norris

Team Falco

Fighting for Esme - Jen Talty

Fighting for Charli - Leanne Tyler

Fighting for Tessa - Stacey Wilk

Fighting for Kora - Deanna L. Rowley

Fighting for Fiona - Kris Norris

Athena Project

Beck's Six - Desiree Holt

Victoria's Six - Delilah Devlin

Cygny's Six - Reina Torres

Fay's Six - Jen Talty

Melody's Six - Regan Black

Team Trojan

Defending Sophie - Desiree Holt

Defending Evangeline - Delilah Devlin

Defending Casey - Reina Torres

Defending Sparrow - Jen Talty

Defending Avery - Regan Black

BROTHERHOOD PROTECTORS
ORIGINAL SERIES BY ELLE JAMES

Brotherhood Protectors International

Athens Affair (#1)

Belgian Betrayal (#2)

Croatia Collateral (#3)

Dublin Debacle (#4)

Edinburgh Escape (#5)

Brotherhood Protectors Hawaii

Kalea's Hero (#1)

Leilani's Hero (#2)

Kiana's Hero (#3)

Maliea's Hero (#4)

Emi's Hero (#5)

Sachie's Hero (#6)

Kimo's Hero (#7)

Alana's Hero (#8)

Nala's Hero (#9)

Mika's Hero (#10)

Bayou Brotherhood Protectors

Remy (#1)

Gerard (#2)

Lucas (#3)

Beau (#4)

Rafael (#5)

Valentin (#6)

Landry (#7)

Simon (#8)

Maurice (#9)

Jacques (#10)

Brotherhood Protectors Yellowstone

Saving Kyla (#1)

Saving Chelsea (#2)

Saving Amanda (#3)

Saving Liliana (#4)

Saving Breely (#5)

Saving Savvie (#6)

Saving Jenna (#7)

Saving Peyton (#8)

Saving Londyn (#9)

Brotherhood Protectors Colorado

SEAL Salvation (#1)

Rocky Mountain Rescue (#2)

Ranger Redemption (#3)

Tactical Takeover (#4)

Colorado Conspiracy (#5)

Rocky Mountain Madness (#6)

Free Fall (#7)

Colorado Cold Case (#8)

Fool's Folly (#9)

Colorado Free Rein (#10)

Rocky Mountain Venom (#11)

High Country Hero (#12)

Brotherhood Protectors

Montana SEAL (#1)

Bride Protector SEAL (#2)

Montana D-Force (#3)

Cowboy D-Force (#4)

Montana Ranger (#5)

Montana Dog Soldier (#6)

Montana SEAL Daddy (#7)

Montana Ranger's Wedding Vow (#8)

Montana SEAL Undercover Daddy (#9)

Cape Cod SEAL Rescue (#10)

Montana SEAL Friendly Fire (#11)

Montana SEAL's Mail-Order Bride (#12)

SEAL Justice (#13)

Ranger Creed (#14)

Delta Force Rescue (#15)

Dog Days of Christmas (#16)

Montana Rescue (#17)

Montana Ranger Returns (#18)

Hot SEAL Salty Dog (SEALs in Paradise)

Hot SEAL,Hawaiian Nights (SEALs in Paradise)

Hot SEAL Bachelor Party (SEALs in Paradise)

Hot SEAL, Independence Day (SEALs in Paradise)

Brotherhood Protectors Boxed Set 1

Brotherhood Protectors Boxed Set 2

Brotherhood Protectors Boxed Set 3

Brotherhood Protectors Boxed Set 4

Brotherhood Protectors Boxed Set 5

Brotherhood Protectors Boxed Set 6

ABOUT ELLE JAMES

ELLE JAMES also writing as MYLA JACKSON is a *New York Times* and *USA Today* Bestselling author of books including cowboys, intrigues and paranormal adventures that keep her readers on the edges of their seats. When she's not at her computer, she's traveling, snow skiing, boating, or riding her ATV, dreaming up new stories. Learn more about Elle James at www.ellejames.com

Website | Facebook | Twitter | GoodReads | Newsletter | BookBub | Amazon

Or visit her alter ego Myla Jackson at
mylajackson.com
Website | Facebook | Twitter | Newsletter

Follow Me!
www.ellejames.com
ellejamesauthor@gmail.com